CHILDREN'S FAVOURITE TALES

Bracken Books

LONDON

First published 1985
by View Productions Pty. Ltd., Sydney.

This edition published 1986 by Bracken Books,
a division of Bestseller Publications Limited, Brent House,
24 Friern Park, London N12 9DA, England.

ISBN 1 85170 007 2

Manufactured by C.T. Products, London, England.

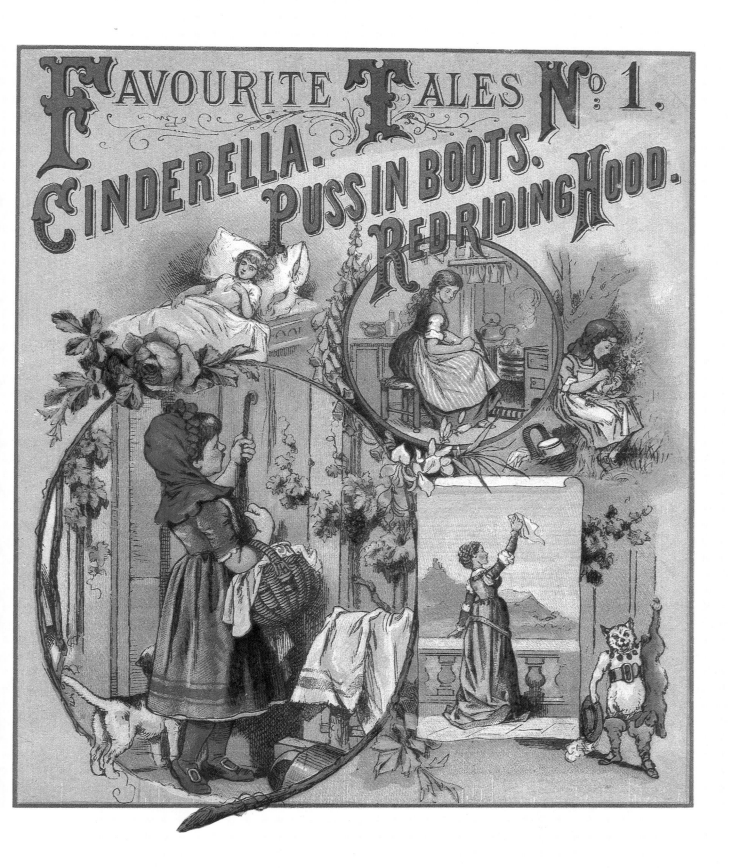

FAVOURITE TALES Nº 1.

CINDERELLA. PUSS IN BOOTS. RED RIDING HOOD.

Cinderella; or, The Glass Slipper.

MANY ages since, there lived a gentleman of fortune and his wife, an amiable and beautiful lady. They were fondly attached to each other, and the birth of a daughter increased their happiness; but, unfortunately for the child, the mother died before she had reared her offspring, and left her husband a prey to sorrow. When the gentleman's grief was a little abated, he resolved to look for some prudent lady, who might be a mother to his child and a companion to himself. Unfortunately, his choice fell on a proud and tyrannical lady, who had two daughters, both equally haughty as their mother. Shortly after the marriage his wife appeared in her true character, and treated his dear girl with great harshness. The gentleman remonstrated against the cruelty of her behaviour, but all to no purpose; and, unable to resist her violence, he fell into low spirits, became ill, and died.

After the death of her father, the young orphan found the hardships of her situation greatly increased. If she came into any of the rooms where her step-mother or step-sisters were, she was sure of being scolded, because the latter were so much vexed that she looked handsomer than themselves. They even went so far as to make her do all the meanest work of the kitchen.

Although so cruelly used, the sweet girl went through all this drudgery without repining; and, when her work was done, she would sit down in the chimney-corner among the cinders; which made the family call her Cinderella. Notwithstanding all this, Cinderella became every day more beautiful, and far surpassed the two sisters, with all their fine clothes.

About this time, a splendid ball was to be given by the King's son, to which all the nobility and gentry were invited, and, among others, the two sisters received an invitation. The two haughty creatures, quite delighted with the thoughts of being at a ball given by the King's son, immediately proceeded to arrange their dresses for the grand occasion. Although these vain, silly girls could chatter enough about fine clothes, yet, in dressing tastefully, they were infinitely surpassed by Cinderella; and as they knew she had a natural genius in these matters, they condescended to employ her on this occasion.

Notwithstanding the attention paid by Cinderella, the ungrateful creatures could not refrain from their accustomed derision, and asked if she would like to go to the ball. "Ah!" said Cinderella, "it is not a place for such poor girls as I am, to go to." "You are right," they said; "how the folks would laugh were they to see a cinder-wench in the ball-room!"

At length the wished-for moment arrived, and these proud misses stepped into their carriage, and drove away to the palace. Cinderella followed the coach with her eyes as far as she could see, and then returned to the kitchen in tears. There she stood until a noise aroused her, and she looked up to see what had occasioned it. Her surprise was great indeed to see a little curious looking woman, with a wand in her hand, who approached and thus accosted her:—

"My dear Cinderella, I am your fairy godmother, and knowing the desire you have to go to this fine ball, I am come for the purpose of gratifying your wish. But you must do as I tell you. First of all, go into the garden and fetch me a pumpkin." Cinderella almost flew to obey her commands, and returned with the finest she could meet with. Her godmother then bade her fetch the rat-trap, in which was a fine large rat, the mouse-trap, which contained six mice, and a couple of lizards: these were placed by the side of the pumpkin, and, the fairy touching them with her wand, they instantly became one of the most elegant of carriages with stately attendants that ever was seen.

"Now, my dear," said the fairy, "is not this as fine an equipage as you could desire?" "O yes, dear godmother," replied Cinderella, "but how can I appear among so many finely-dressed people in these mean-looking clothes?"

"Give yourself no uneasiness about that, my dear," said the fairy, touching Cinderella with her magic wand, and her clothes were instantly changed into magnificent apparel, ornamented with the most costly jewels that ever were beheld. The fairy took from her pocket a beautiful pair of elastic glass slippers, which she caused Cinderella to put on, and then desired her to get into the carriage at once, as the ball had already commenced; but she strictly charged her on no account whatever to stay at the ball after the clock had struck twelve; and then added that if she did so, her fine coach, horses, coachman, footmen, and her fine apparel, would all return to their original states.

Cinderella promised most faithfully to attend to everything that the fairy had mentioned; and then, quite overjoyed, drove away to the palace. The arrival of so splendid an equipage as Cinderella's could not fail to attract notice;

and the King's son, hearing that a beautiful young princess was in waiting, hastened to hand her out of the carriage, and led her gracefully into the ball-room. The King's son conducted Cinderella to one of the most distinguished seats, and placing himself by her side, handed her some refreshments. He then requested to have the honour of dancing with her. Cinderella gave a smiling consent, and the delighted prince led her into the ball-room, followed by the eyes of the whole company. A magnificent collation was served up, but the young prince was too much engaged in attending to Cinderella to eat a morsel during the whole evening. The two sisters were seated close to her; and such was her goodness of heart, that she even gave them a part of the fine delicacies which she had received from the prince. Cinderella hearing the clock strike a quarter to twelve, at once rose, and took a hurried leave of the company.

Next evening, the two sisters went again to the ball, and Cinderella too. The prince was quite delighted to see her again, and did not leave her the whole evening; but Cinderella so enjoyed herself that the clock struck twelve when she supposed it could scarcely be eleven. Alarmed, she almost flew from the ball-room. The prince pursued her, and in the hurry she dropped one of her glass slippers, which he picked up.

A few days after the ball, it was proclaimed that the prince would marry the lady whom the slipper fitted. It was carried to all the great ladies, but without success; so the prince ordered it to be taken to the other single ladies of his dominions, and it was brought at last to the two sisters, who tried to squeeze the slipper on, but all to no purpose. Cinderella asked if she might try it on, and, in spite of the laughter of her two sisters, she was allowed to do so. To their great astonishment, it fitted her exactly; but they were much more astonished when she pulled its fellow from her pocket, and put it on likewise. At that moment the fairy entered unperceived, and touching Cinderella with her wand, changed her clothes into the beautiful dress she had worn at the ball. The prince's officer at once conducted her to his master, who was so overjoyed to see his princess again, that he at once asked her hand in marriage.

Cinderella gave her consent, and the ceremony took place a short time afterwards with great pomp and rejoicing. She freely forgave her sisters all their unkindnesses, and lived for many happy years loved and respected by everybody for her many amiable qualities.

PUSS IN BOOTS;
Or, THE MILLER'S SON.

HERE once lived a miller who had three sons. On his death-bed, he called them together and divided his property among them. To the eldest he gave his mill and land, to the second his donkey and sacks, but to the third he left only a Cat.

The youngest could not tell what he could do with a Cat to get his living; and the day after his father's death, as he was sitting with Pussy bewailing his hard fate, he said, "Ah! I fear we shall have to starve."

Much to his surprise, however, the Cat suddenly found speech, and thus answered: "Pray do not grieve at your fate, but put your trust in me, and you shall be richer than both your brothers. Give me a bag, get me a handsome pair of boots, do as I wish you, and leave the rest to me!"

His master, thinking no great harm could come of Pussy's request, got him the required articles; and no sooner had Puss got the boots and the bag than he started out to a rabbit-warren known only to himself, and, baiting the bag with parsley, soon caught six large rabbits. With these he went straight off to court to see the King, and gaining audience of his Majesty, with a graceful bow, said—"Please, your Majesty, I have brought this bag of game from my master, the Marquis of Carabas, who desires me to lay it with most loyal respect at your feet."

The King received him graciously, and told him to convey his best thanks to the Marquis for so very acceptable a present.

Soon after this, Puss persuaded his master to bathe in the river just about the time the King and the Princess, his daughter, were taking their morning ride. Puss cunningly hid his master's clothes, and then called out—"Oh! oh! my Lord of Carabas is drowning; some thief has stolen his clothes!"

His Majesty at once sent for a grand suit from the court, in which the miller's son was soon dressed. He was then invited to accompany them to the palace, where the pretended Marquis so pleased the King and his daughter, that they requested him to stay several days.

Puss, knowing that an Ogre, a magician, lived some few miles off—who was possessed of much property and could change himself into any animal at will—at once set off to his stronghold; and, after travelling all night and all day, came to the castle. Giving a rat-a-tat-tat at the gate, Puss informed the Ogre that the King had heard of his wonderful powers, and had sent him to see if it was all true, before he came with his whole retinue to visit him.

The Ogre was so delighted at being thus taken notice of, that he said he would show the cat his skill; so he at once transformed himself into a lion. Not at all dismayed, Pussy bowed to him as king of beasts, and said, "It is all very grand for you to change yourself into a large animal, like a lion; but I should say it was impossible for you to change yourself into so small a one as a mouse."

The Ogre, to prove what his powers were, at once changed himself into a mouse; and Puss, watching his opportunity, sprang upon him and in an instant ate him up.

Pussy then informed the Ogre's servants in the castle as well as those he found working in the fields, that their master in future meant taking the form of a Prince, and sent out cards of invitation to all the nobility round about as from the "Marquis of Carabas."

He then went back to the palace, and told his master all that he had done, and persuaded him to grandly receive the King, the Princess, and court, at the castle that was now his own.

His Majesty was delighted to find the Marquis so rich, and made him one of his chief ministers, so that he was in constant attendance at court. The Princess, meanwhile, had fallen deeply in love with the Marquis, once the miller's son; and, after a short courtship, they were married in great pomp and state. Puss, you may rest assured, was well taken care of during the remainder of his lifetime.

LITTLE RED RIDING HOOD.

MANY years ago, in a village there lived a sweet-tempered little girl, whose parents loved her very dearly; but her Grandmother quite doated on her, and made her a pretty red-coloured hood. You may be sure that the child looked quite charming in it. "What do you say for it?" said her Grandmother, as she looked lovingly at the little maiden, who answered her with many kisses, and said, "Now I have this fine new cloak, Grandmother, people will call me LITTLE RED RIDING HOOD."

One day, her mother having made some cheesecakes, said to her, "Your Grandmother is ill, I fear, so carry her this pot of fresh-made butter and a few of these cheesecakes; but, mind, do not stop to talk with any one you meet on the road, and come back before sundown."

Little Red Riding Hood set out for her Grandmother's cottage. As she was crossing a thick wood, which lay in her road, she met a Wolf, who had a great mind to eat her, but dared not, because of some woodcutters who were at work near them. So, wagging his tail he asked her where she was going. Not knowing how dangerous it was to talk to a Wolf, and quite forgetting her mother's advice, she said, "I am going to see my Grandmother, to take her these cakes and this pot of butter." "Does she live far off?" said the Wolf. "Oh, yes!" said Little Red Riding Hood; "beyond the mill, which you see yonder, at the very first house you come to in the village."

Away went the Wolf running at full speed, taking the nearest road; but the little girl did not hurry there, for she amused herself with singing songs, and gathering wild flowers which grew in the wood, which she made up into a pretty nosegay for her Grandmother.

The Wolf, who had run all the way, soon arrived at the cottage of Red Riding Hood's Grandmother, and knocked at the door.

"Who's there?" asked the Grandmother.

"It is your grandchild, Red Riding Hood," said the Wolf, trying to imitate her voice; "mother has sent you some cheesecakes and a pot of fresh butter."

The good old woman, who was ill in bed, called out, "Pull the bobbin, and the door will open." Accordingly, the Wolf did as he was told, opened the door and entered the cottage, where he found all very quiet; so he softly closed the door after him, and stealthily crept towards the bed where the good old lady was laying; for she was too unwell to dress herself that morning.

Alas! poor old woman, instead of beholding her pretty grandchild, it was a ravenous and wicked Wolf, who, not having tasted any food for three days, sprang upon her, and ate her up. Then he put on the old lady's night-cap and bed-gown, looked at himself in the glass, smiled, and went to bed, to wait for the little girl's arrival.

He listened to every sound that broke the silence; for he thought that every footstep must be that of Little Red Riding Hood. At last he felt rather drowsy after his hearty meal and would have gone to sleep, but fear of any stranger coming to the cottage kept him awake. In about an hour, however, Little Red Riding Hood came, and gently tapped at the door.

"Who is there?" said the Wolf. She replied—supposing that it was her Grandmother who spoke—"It is I, your own grandchild, Little Riding Hood. Mother has sent you some cheesecakes and a pot of nice fresh butter."

The Wolf, softening his voice as much as he possibly could, as well as trying to imitate the Grandmother's voice, said, "Pull the bobbin, and the door will open." Having pulled the bobbin, Red Riding Hood went into the house; when the Wolf said softly, "Put the basket down, my dear child, and come into bed with me; for you must be very tired."

"Yes, I will, Grandmother," said the poor little innocent, "as soon as I have put these pretty flowers, which I have gathered for you, into the pots. See, dear Grandmother, how nicely I have decorated your chimney-piece."

The Wolf, however, declined looking at the flowers, pretending that his head ached so sadly that he could not raise it.

"I am very sorry you are so ill," said Little Red Riding Hood, "and mother will be much grieved to hear it. Shall I hand you some nice cake?"

"No, thank you, my dear," answered the Wolf, "I cannot eat just now, I do not feel at all hungry." Little Red Riding Hood soon after this got into bed, but declined taking her dress off; and in talking said, "Do you know, Grandmother, as I came along, I met a Wolf in the wood: at first I was frightened, but he spoke so kindly that my fears soon ended. I hope you are not angry with me for speaking to him."

"No," said the Wolf, slyly, "not at all."

Little Red Riding Hood being tired from her walk, soon fell asleep. The Wolf was so pleased at having her in his power, that in pressing her rather tightly she awoke, and thinking how very much altered her Grandmother looked, she could not help saying, "How rough and long your arms have grown!" "The better to fondle you with, my dear child." "But, Grandmother, how your ears stand up!" "The better to hear your sweet voice, my love." "How large and bright your eyes are, Grandmother!" "The better to gaze upon you, my love." "But how huge and frightful your teeth are!" "All the better to——"

The Wolf was going to say—"Better to eat you with," and was about to seize the little girl, when suddenly there was the bark of a dog outside and the voices of men. The next minute, in rushed Red Riding Hood's father.

The old Wolf leaped out of bed, and tried to escape; but Red Riding Hood's father gave him a sharp rap over the nose and sent him back again. "Kill the Wolf! kill him!" said all the men together. But Little Red Riding Hood's father said, "No; let us do better than that. Let us sell him to the master of a wild beast show."

Little Red Riding Hood was very sorry that she had disobeyed her mother and talked with a stranger by the way, when she was told not to do so. She never did so again. As for the Wolf, he was sold for a lump of money, which was safely kept and given to Red Riding Hood on her twenty-first birthday.

By this story we may see how very wrong it is for children not to do exactly as they are desired by their parents; and, even by a little error, what great evil and suffering they bring upon themselves, and upon those they love.

Favourite Tales No. 2.
Blue Beard. Sleeping Beauty.
Hop-o-my Thumb.

BLUE BEARD.

IN a grand old castle in the East, some thousand years ago, there dwelt a wealthy man, possessed of immense riches, and beautiful gardens, groves and fields; but with all his wealth and stately dwelling, there was one great peculiarity about him, and that was, he had the misfortune to possess a beard of a blue tint; consequently he was called BLUE BEARD for miles and miles around.

Now, I must tell you that this man had married a great number of ladies, but they had all disappeared mysteriously; and as he led a very secluded life, no one knew what became of them; and the people round about, being his tenants, dared not hint at anything unfair respecting his conduct.

There came to reside near to his castle an estimable family, consisting of an elderly lady and her two daughters; both these young ladies were highly accomplished and much admired, but the younger of the two was thought to be unusually handsome, and was therefore noticed rather more than her sister. It often happens that beauty is a misfortune; because, if a young lady has not good sense as well as beauty, it will make her vain; and a vain girl often falls into misery or trouble. There were also two sons, who were at this time away at the wars.

Blue Beard, becoming acquainted with the family, invited the lady's two daughters to his mansion. After a short time the young ladies set out for the castle, and at length reached the gate that led through the grounds. Although they had heard a great deal of the taste and expense lavished to improve and decorate the land around the castle, yet they were surprised by the many unexpected beauties of nature which met their view. Having passed through these delightful grounds, they were met by Blue Beard himself at the entrance hall, with a retinue of servants. They ascended the grand staircase and proceeded into a drawing-room that completely surpassed all their ideas of grandeur.

Blue Beard paid great attention to the sisters, more especially to the youngest, whose name was Fatima, and after a short courtship married her. The marriage ceremony was one of great splendour, and all went on happily for awhile; Ann, Fatima's sister, residing at the castle with her.

One day, Blue Beard, pretending that he had a long journey to undertake, left with his wife the keys of the castle, telling her by no means to enter the blue chamber at the end of the gallery, at the same time observing she might have access to any other room the castle contained.

Fatima promised that she would obey his desire, and said that she would not disappoint the confidence he had placed in her: and shortly after his departure the two sisters began to view the apartments. They went from room to room until at last they had seen into all of them except the blue chamber. After hesitating some time, they summoned up courage to enter that also. Fatima entered first, and was horrified at the sight which met her view; for there were several headless bodies of ladies within the chamber. In her fright she dropped the key in a pool of blood, but picked it up hurriedly and rushed distractedly from the room.

Fatima and her sister tried to wash the blood off the key, but in vain. In spite of all their efforts, they could not get the key clean, and Fatima waited with dread the return of her husband.

When Blue Beard came home, she was making a last attempt to wash off the stains, and he caught her in the very act. He at once charged her with entering the forbidden chamber, for which she would have to suffer death. The wretched girl fell on her knees, the tears rushed from her eyes, and unable to speak, supplicantly implored his mercy. But all would not do: Blue Beard, standing with his sword unsheathed, gave her but a quarter of an hour to prepare for death. Sister Ann, who was almost petrified at the sight, gave a

dreadful shriek when she saw the instrument of death raised over her defenceless sister, and which for a moment delayed the treacherous weapon.

Poor Fatima begged of her sister to at once ascend the tower and see if their brothers were coming, as she expected them on a visit; but Ann could not see anyone on the road. Blue Beard was now getting very impatient, and in a loud voice commanded Fatima to come down immediately. She pleaded a few moments longer, and cried once again to her sister,—"Ann, sister Ann, do you see anyone coming?" Her reply was, "Only some sheep making a cloud of dust." Again, as Blue Beard called out, "The time is more than up, I will not wait longer!" she cried out, "Ann! dear sister Ann! oh, see if our brothers are coming!" Her reply was, "There now appear to be two horsemen on the road!"

Blue Beard, losing all patience, rushed at poor Fatima, and dragged her down by her beautiful hair. He then drew his sabre and was about to cut off her head, when the brothers, who had seen their sister so anxiously waving her handkerchief on top of the castle, put spur to their horses, rushed into the castle, and stabbed him to the heart.

Fatima's first care was to have the bodies of all the unfortunate ladies of the blue chamber decently buried and all traces of that apartment cleared away. She then set about seeing to the poor of the neighbourhood, making their cottages in every way comfortable, and adding to each a plot of ground; so that, in a very short time, every one was made happy and became her firm friends and supporters.

SLEEPING BEAUTY.

MANY, many years ago, there lived a King and Queen who had no children, which made them very unhappy. Hoping by some means or other to have an heir, they agreed to consult all the fairies they could hear of; and some time after this a Princess was born. The christening was most sumptuous, and seven fairies were invited to be her godmothers; so that each might bestow upon her a gift, as was the custom in those days.

When the ceremony of baptism was over, a splendid entertainment was prepared for the fairies; before each of whom was set a magnificent cover of massive gold, with knife, fork, and spoon, set with diamonds and rubies, all of the most curious workmanship.

As the company were about to place themselves at the table, an old fairy, who had been forgotten for many years, entered the banquet-room. The King immediately ordered a cover to be brought for her, but it could not be of massive gold, because only seven had been made.

The old fairy, seeing that her cover was not so handsome as those of the other fairies, muttered that she would be revenged. A young fairy, who sat near and heard her, resolved to prevent, as far at she could, the harm intended by the old fairy. The fairies now began to bestow gifts on the infant Princess: the first said that she should be most beautiful; the second, that she should be very witty; the third, that she should have enchanting grace; the fourth, that she should dance delightfully; the fifth, that she should sing like a nightingale; and the sixth that she should excel in playing on every musical instrument.

The old fairy now stepped forward and said, "The Princess shall pierce her hand with a spindle and die of the wound." The young fairy, who had concealed herself till now, advanced and said, "Do not afflict yourselves, O King and Queen, the Princess shall not die of her wound; she shall only sleep for a hundred years, at the end of which time she shall be awakened by an amiable young Prince."

The King, anxious to prevent injury to his daughter, caused it to be proclaimed that no person should hereafter use a spindle.

As the Princess grew up, all the graces bestowed upon her began to show themselves, and she became more and more engaging. One day, the old fairy, who had transformed herself into a frog, persuaded her to enter an old apartment in a remote part of the palace, where an old lady sat using a spindle. The Princess, never having seen one before, took hold of it, and the end pierced her hand; on which she instantly fell into a profound sleep. She was at once removed to her own apartment and laid on a couch. The kind fairy now appeared, and waving her wand, caused every person in the palace to fall asleep, so that they might awake with the Princess, and be ready to attend her when her long sleep was over.

Many years passed away, and a dense forest grew around the palace, which quite hid it from view. When the hundred years had elapsed, a Prince and his followers were hunting near the spot; and as he came near to the trees, they separated to let him pass. Onward he passed, the trees closing after him, and at last he arrived at the palace gates. He entered, but the silence which reigned within quite startled him; however, he took courage and passed through several rooms, in which every person he saw was fast asleep. At length the Prince entered a splendid apartment, where lay on an elegant couch the most beautiful lady he had ever beheld. With intense admiration he gazed upon her for some time, and falling on one knee, he gently took the hand of the Princess and pressed it to his lips.

The enchantment was now ended; the Princess opened her eyes, and with a look of tenderness said, "Ah! dear Prince, it was you who was my companion during my long sleep. I very well knew that he who should end my enchantment would be the handsomest of men, and that he would love me even more than he loved himself; and the moment I saw you, I recollected your face."

The King, Queen, and attendants awoke at the same time, and commenced their several duties as if nothing had happened. The Prince assisted the Princess to rise. She was magnificently dressed; but he wisely did not tell her that her clothes were in the style of those worn by his great-grandmother; however, they became her so well that she looked exceedingly beautiful.

The Prince and Princess passed the evening greatly delighted with each other's company, and her parents agreed that the chaplain should marry them that night. The ceremony accordingly took place; and the next day the Prince conducted his bride, accompanied by her attendants, to his father's palace. The King and Queen most lovingly received their handsome daughter; and, of this we may rest assured, that the Prince and his beautiful wife passed a long and happy life.

HOP - O' - MY - THUMB.

HOP-O'-MY-THUMB was the youngest of seven boys, all diminutive and delicate little fellows, whose parents were poor faggot-cutters and wood-gatherers. He was such a little fellow that the family called him by the above name,—and so will we. Being also a very quiet boy, he was made the drudge of the family; still, although so small, he was very clever.

It happened just at this time that for want of rain the crops were bad, and there was a famine throughout the country; and as the parents of Hop-o'-my-Thumb and his brothers could not bear to see the children starve before their eyes, they decided, since they could think of no other remedy, to leave them in a thick wood a long way off. Hop-o'-my-Thumb one evening hearing his parents talking over what should be done with them, resolved to save himself and his brothers; so he rose early the next morning and filled his pockets with small white pebbles, and when their father and mother led them away, he dropped the pebbles by the wayside as he went along.

When their parents, after cutting a few bundles of faggots, left them in the thickest part of the wood, the children began to cry bitterly; but Hop-o'-my-Thumb was, by the aid of the stones he had dropped, able to lead his brothers home again. Meanwhile, a gentleman had sent the faggot-maker and his wife a small amount of money due to them; and as they were going out to purchase provisions and endeavour to find their children, both mother and father were gratified to see them return. But, as this money did not last very long, and they could not bear to see their children starve, a few days later on they gave them each a piece of bread and took them forth again, this time resolving to leave them in a darker and thicker part of the forest. Hop-o'-my-Thumb strewed crumbs by the way as he did the stones, but the poor hungry

birds came and picked them up, and so the poor brothers could not again retrace their steps.

The children, finding themselves deserted, wandered on and on until they came to an open plain; and at last, seeing a light in the distance, they turned towards it, and presently found themselves in front of a large castle. Knocking at the door, it was opened by a comely dame, who said she could not give them shelter, as her husband was an Ogre and would eat them up. They begged so hard, Hop-o'-my-Thumb saying they were poor and hungry children who had lost their way, that at last the Ogress let them in, and, after giving them a good supper, put them to bed in the same room in which her seven daughters slept, putting on each boy a red night-cap.

Soon the Ogre arrived home, and when he had eaten an immense supper and drank a large quantity of wine, he began to sniff about and cried out, "I smell children's flesh!" and immediately went to the bed-room and dragged out little Hop-o'-my-Thumb. He was about to kill him, but his wife advised him, having had a good supper, to rest contented until the morning.

Now, you must know, the Ogre had seven daughters, and each wore a crown of gold upon her head when she slept. Hop-o'-my-Thumb perceiving this—as they slept in the same room—thought that perhaps the Ogre would kill him and his brothers in the night; so, as softly as he could, he got out of bed in the dead of the night and changed his own and his brothers' caps for the girls' crowns.

Soon afterwards the monster came into the room, and feeling the heads of the boys, found the crowns upon them; he then went to the other bed, and feeling the night-caps said, "Oh! there you are my lads!" and unkowningly cut the throats of his seven daughters, one by one.

Early next morning, Hop-o'-my-Thumb and his brothers slipped out of the house, and started they knew not whither, running for many miles with all their strength.

When the Ogre awoke the next morning and found out what he had done, he at once put on his seven-league boots and started in pursuit. After striding over different parts of the country, he at last entered the road which the

children had taken, and Hop-o'-my-Thumb perceiving a hole in a rock, at once took shelter therein.

The Ogre, feeling tired, lay down to sleep on the very rock under which the children were concealed, before he had sniffed or seen them. As soon as he was sound asleep and snoring, Hop-o'-my-Thumb started his brothers off home, climbed the rock, and took off the Ogre's boots—which being magical would fit any one—and put them on himself.

A fairy then appeared, who told him that the castle and its contents belonged of right to his parents and their family; for the wicked Ogre had by false means obtained possession of the estate, money, and jewels. By her command he went to the castle, knocked loudly at the door, and told the Ogress, who was greatly startled to see him again, that she was to give him the great key and come with him to the King, telling her that she was to be made a lady at Court. She fetched the key very briskly and gave it to Hop-o'-my-Thumb, informing him at the same time where he could find the chest of money and jewels to which it belonged, whereupon he took as much as he could carry home to his parents. He and the Ogress then proceeded on their way; and as they passed beneath the rock they saw the lifeless body of the Ogre, who in his heavy sleep had fallen over and shattered all his limbs.

The Ogress, although deeply grieved at the loss of her little ones, did not regret the death of the cruel Ogre, and was placed in comfort by Hop-o'-my-Thumb for the rest of her life.

The fame of Hop-o'-my-Thumb and his wonderful boots soon reached the King, who immediately sent for him; and he became of great service to the state in carrying messages rapidly to and from the battle-field.

Hop-o'-my-Thumb every day grew more brave and witty, until at last the King made him the greatest lord in the kingdom, and put all his affairs under his direction. Having recovered the castle and all connected with it, he was able to keep his parents and brothers in a good position for the remainder of their days.

The Christmas Cuckoo.

ONCE upon a time there stood in the midst of a bleak moor, in the north country, a certain village; all its inhabitants were poor, for their fields were barren, and they had little trade, but the poorest of them all were two brothers called Scrub and Spare, who followed the cobbler's craft, and had but one stall between them. It was a hut built of clay and wattles. The door was low and always open, for there was no window. The roof did not entirely keep out the rain, and the only thing comfortable about it was a wide hearth, for which the brothers could never find wood enough to make a sufficient fire. There they worked in most brotherly friendship, though with little encouragement.

"The people of that village were not extravagant in shoes, and better cobblers than Scrub and Spare might be found. Spiteful people said there were no shoes so bad that they would not be worse for their mending. Nevertheless Scrub and Spare managed to live between their own trade, a small barley field, and a cottage garden, till one unlucky day when a new cobbler arrived in the village. He had lived in the capital city of the kingdom, and, by his own account, cobbled for the queen and the princesses. His awls were sharp, his lasts were new; he set up his stall in a neat cottage with two windows. The villagers soon found out that one patch of his would wear two of the brothers'. In short, all the mending left Scrub and Spare, and went to the new cobbler. The season had been wet and cold, their barley did not ripen well, and the cabbages never half closed in the garden. So the brothers were poor that winter, and when Christmas came they had nothing to feast on but a barley loaf, a piece of rusty bacon, and some small beer of their own

brewing. Worse than that, the snow was very deep, and they could get no firewood. Their hut stood at the end of the village, beyond it spread the bleak moor, now all white and silent; but that moor had once been a forest, great roots of old trees were still to be found in it, loosened from the soil and laid bare by the winds and rains—one of these, a rough, gnarled log, lay hard by their door, the half of it above the snow, and Spare said to his brother—

"'Shall we sit here cold on Christmas while the great root lies yonder? Let us chop it up for firewood, the work will make us warm.'

"'No,' said Scrub; 'it's not right to chop wood on Christmas; besides, that root is too hard to be broken with any hatchet.'

"'Hard or not we must have a fire,' replied Spare. 'Come, brother, help me in with it. Poor as we are, there is nobody in the village will have such a yule log as ours.'

"Scrub liked a little grandeur, and in hopes of having a fine yule log, both brothers strained and strove with all their might till, between pulling and pushing, the great old root was safe on the hearth, and beginning to crackle and blaze with the red embers. In high glee, the cobblers sat down to their beer and bacon. The door was shut, for there was nothing but cold moonlight and snow outside; but the hut, strewn with fir boughs, and ornamented with holly, looked cheerful as the ruddy blaze flared up and rejoiced their hearts.

"'Long life and good fortune to ourselves, brother!' said Spare. 'I hope you will drink that toast, and may we never have a worse fire on Christmas—but what is that?'

"Spare set down the drinking-horn, and the brothers listened astonished, for out of the blazing root they heard, 'Cuckoo! cuckoo!' as plain as ever the spring-bird's voice came over the moor on a May morning.

"'It is something bad,' said Scrub, terribly frightened.

"'May be not,' said Spare; and out of the deep hole at the side which the fire had not reached flew a large grey cuckoo, and lit on the table before them. Much as the cobblers had been surprised, they were still more so when it said—

"'Good gentlemen, what season is this?'

"'It's Christmas,' said Spare.

"'Then a merry Christmas to you!' said the cuckoo. 'I went to sleep in the hollow of that old root one evening last summer, and never woke till the heat of your fire made me think it was summer again; but now since you have burned my lodging, let me stay in your hut till the spring comes round—I only want a hole to sleep in, and when I go on my travels next summer be assured I will bring you some present for your trouble.'

"'Stay, and welcome,' said Spare, while Scrub sat wondering if it were something bad or not; 'I'll make you a good warm hole in the thatch. But you must be hungry after that long sleep?—here is a slice of barley bread. Come, help us to keep Christmas!'

"The cuckoo ate up the slice, drank water from the brown jug, for he would take no beer, and flew into a snug hole which Spare scooped for him in the thatch of the hut.

"Scrub said he was afraid it wouldn't be lucky; but as it slept on, and the days passed, he forgot his fears. So the snow melted, the heavy rains came, the cold grew less, the days lengthened, and one sunny morning the brothers were awoke by the cuckoo shouting its own cry to let them know the spring had come.

"'Now I'm going on my travels,' said the bird, 'over the world to tell men of the spring. There is no country where trees bud or flowers bloom, that I will not cry in before the year goes round. Give me another slice of barley bread to keep me on my journey, and tell me what present I shall bring you at the twelvemonth's end.'

"Scrub would have been angry with his brother for cutting so large a slice, their store of barley-meal being low; but his mind was occupied with what present would be most prudent to ask: at length a lucky thought struck him.

"'Good master cuckoo,' said he, 'if a great traveller who sees all the world like you, could know of any place where diamonds or pearls were to be found, one of a tolerable size brought in your beak would help such poor men as my brother and I to provide something better than barley bread for your next entertainment.'

"'I know nothing of diamonds or pearls,' said the cuckoo; 'they are in the hearts of rocks and the sands of rivers. My knowledge is only of that which grows on the earth. But there are two trees hard by the well that lies at the world's end—one of them is called the golden tree, for its leaves are all of beaten gold: every winter they fall into the well with a sound like scattered coin, and I know not what becomes of them. As for the other, it is always green like a laurel. Some call it the wise, and some the merry tree. Its leaves never fall, but they that get one of them keep a blythe heart in spite of all misfortunes, and can make themselves as merry in a hut as in a palace.'

"'Good master cuckoo, bring me a leaf off that tree!' cried Spare.

"'Now, brother, don't be a fool!' said Scrub; 'think of the leaves of beaten gold! Dear master cuckoo, bring me one of them!'

"Before another word could be spoken, the cuckoo had flown out of the open door, and was shouting its spring cry over moor and meadow.

The brothers were poorer than ever that year; nobody would send them a single shoe to mend. The new cobbler said, in scorn, they should come to be his apprentices; and Scrub and Spare would have left the village but for their barley field, their cabbage garden, and a certain maid called Fairfeather, whom both the cobblers had courted for seven years without even knowing which she meant to favour.

"Sometimes Fairfeather seemed inclined to Scrub, sometimes she smiled on Spare; but the brothers never disputed for that. They sowed their barley, planted their cabbage, and now that their trade was gone, worked in the rich villagers' fields to make out a scanty living. So the seasons came and passed: spring, summer, harvest, and winter followed each other as they have done from the beginning. At the end of the latter, Scrub and Spare had grown so poor and ragged that Fairfeather thought them beneath her notice. Old neighbours forgot to invite them to wedding feasts or merrymaking; and they thought the cuckoo had forgotten them too, when at daybreak, on the first of April, they heard a hard beak knocking at their door, and a voice crying—

"'Cuckoo! cuckoo! Let me in with my presents.'

"Spare ran to open the door, and in came the cuckoo, carrying on one side of his bill a golden leaf larger than that of any tree in the north country; and in the other, one like that of the common laurel, only it had a fresher green.

"'Here,' it said, giving the gold to Scrub and the green to Spare, 'it is a long carriage from the world's end. Give me a slice of barley bread, for I must tell the north country that the spring has come.'

"Scrub did not grudge the thickness of that slice, though it was cut from their last loaf. So much gold had never been in the cobbler's hands before, and he could not help exulting over his brother.

"'See the wisdom of my choice!' he said, holding up the large leaf of gold. 'As for yours, as good might be plucked from any hedge. I wonder a sensible bird would carry the like so far.'

"'Good master cobbler,' cried the cuckoo, finishing the slice, 'your conclusions are more hasty than courteous. If your brother be disappointed this time, I go on the same journey every year, and for your hospitable entertainment will think it no trouble to bring each of you whichever leaf you desire.'

"'Darling cuckoo!' cried Scrub, 'bring me a golden one;' and Spare, looking up from the green leaf on which he gazed as though it were a crown-jewel, said—

"'Be sure to bring me one from the merry tree,' and away flew the cuckoo.

"'This is the Feast of All Fools, and it ought to be your birthday,' said Scrub. 'Did ever man fling away such an opportunity of getting rich! Much good your merry leaves will do in the midst of rags and poverty!' So he went on, but Spare laughed at him, and answered with quaint old proverbs concerning the cares that come with gold, till Scrub, at length getting angry, vowed his brother was not fit to live with a respectable man; and taking his lasts, his awls, and his golden leaf, he left the wattle hut, and went to tell the villagers.

"They were astonished at the folly of Spare, and charmed with Scrub's good sense, particularly when he showed them the golden leaf, and told that the cuckoo would bring him one every spring. The new cobbler immediately took him into partnership; the greatest people sent him their shoes to mend; Fairfeather smiled graciously upon him, and in the course of that summer they were married, with a grand wedding feast, at which the whole village danced, except Spare, who was not invited, because the bride could not bear his low-mindedness, and his brother thought him a disgrace to the family.

"Indeed, all who heard the story concluded that Spare must be mad, and nobody would associate with him but a lame tinker, a beggar-boy, and a poor woman reputed to be a witch because she was old and ugly. As for Scrub, he established himself with Fairfeather in a cottage close by that of the new cobbler, and quite as fine. There he mended shoes to everybody's satisfaction, had a scarlet coat for holidays, and a fat goose for dinner every wedding-day. Fairfeather, too, had a crimson gown and fine blue ribands; but neither she nor Scrub were content, for to buy this grandeur the golden leaf had to be broken and parted with piece by piece, so the last morsel was gone before the cuckoo came with another.

"Spare lived on in the old hut, and worked in the cabbage garden. (Scrub had got the barley field because he was the eldest.) Every day his coat grew more ragged, and the hut more weatherbeaten; but people remarked that he never looked sad nor sour; and the wonder was, that from the time they began to keep his company, the tinker grew kinder to the poor ass with which he travelled the country, the beggar-boy kept out of mischief, and the old woman was never cross to her cat or angry with the children.

"Every first of April the cuckoo came tapping at their doors with the golden leaf to Scrub and the green to Spare. Fairfeather would have entertained him nobly with wheaten bread and honey, for she had some notion of persuading him to bring two gold leaves instead of one; but the cuckoo flew away to eat barley bread with Spare, saying he was not fit company for fine people, and liked the old hut where he slept so snugly from Christmas till Spring.

"Scrub spent the golden leaves, and Spare kept the merry ones; and I know not how many years passed in this manner, when a certain great lord, who owned that village came to the neighbourhood. His castle stood on the moor. It was ancient and strong, with high towers and a deep moat. All the country, as far as one could see from the highest turret, belonged to its lord; but he had not been there for twenty years, and would not have come then, only he was melancholy. The cause of his grief was that he had been prime-minister at court, and in high favour, till somebody told the crown-prince that he had spoken disrespectfully concerning the turning out of his royal highness's toes, and the king that he did not lay on taxes enough, whereon the north country lord was turned out of office, and banished to his own estate. There he lived for some weeks in very bad temper. The servants said nothing would please him, and the villagers put on their worst clothes lest he should raise their rents; but one day in the harvest time his lordship chanced to meet Spare gathering watercresses at a meadow stream, and fell into talk with the cobbler.

"How it was nobody could tell, but from the hour of that discourse the great lord cast away his melancholy: he forgot his lost office and his court enemies, the king's taxes and the crown-prince's toes, and went about with a noble train hunting, fishing, and making merry in his hall, where all travellers were entertained, and all the poor were welcome. This strange story spread through the north country, and great company came to the cobbler's hut—rich men who had lost their money, poor men who had lost their friends, beauties who had grown old, wits who had gone out of fashion, all came to talk with Spare, and whatever their troubles had been, all went home merry. The rich

gave him presents, the poor gave him thanks. Spare's coat ceased to be ragged, he had bacon with his cabbage, and the villagers began to think there was some sense in him.

"By this time his fame had reached the capital city, and even the court. There were a great many discontented people there besides the king, who had lately fallen into ill-humour, because a neighbouring princess, with seven islands for her dowry, would not marry his eldest son. So a royal messenger was sent to Spare, with a velvet mantle, a diamond ring, and a command that he should repair to court immediately.

"'To-morrow is the first of April,' said Spare, 'and I will go with you two hours after sunrise.'

"The messenger lodged all night at the castle, and the cuckoo came at sunrise with the merry leaf.

"'Court is a fine place,' he said when the cobbler told him he was going; 'but I cannot come there, they would lay snares and catch me; so be careful of the leaves I have brought you, and give me a farewell slice of barley bread.'

"Spare was sorry to part with the cuckoo, little as he had of his company; but he gave him a slice which would have broken Scrub's heart in former times, it was so thick and large; and having sewed up the leaves in the lining of his leather doublet, he set out with the messenger on his way to court."

The Christmas Cuckoo—(*continued*).

"HIS coming caused great surprise there. Everybody wondered what the king could see in such a common-looking man; but scarce had his majesty conversed with him half an hour, when the princess and her seven islands were forgotten, and orders given that a feast for all comers should be spread in the banquet hall. The princes of the blood, the great lords and ladies, ministers of state, and judges of the land, after that discoursed with Spare, and the more they talked the lighter grew their hearts, so that such changes had never been seen at court. The lords forgot their spites and the ladies their envies, the princes and ministers made friends among themselves, and the judges showed no favour.

"As for Spare he had a chamber assigned him in the palace, and a seat at the king's table; one sent him rich robes and another costly jewels; but in the midst of all his grandeur he still wore the leathern doublet, which the palace servants thought remarkably mean. One day the king's attention being drawn to it by the chief page, his majesty inquired why Spare didn't give it to a beggar? But the cobbler answered—

"'High and mighty monarch, this doublet was with me before silk and velvet came—I find it easier to wear than the court cut; moreover, it serves to keep me humble, by recalling the days when it was my holiday garment.'

"The king thought this a wise speech, and commanded that no one should find fault with the leathern doublet. So things went, till tidings of his brother's good fortune reached Scrub in the moorland cottage on another first of April, when the cuckoo came with two golden leaves, because he had none to carry for Spare.

"'Think of that!' said Fairfeather. 'Here we are spending our lives in this humdrum place, and Spare making his fortune at court with two or three paltry green leaves! What would they say to our golden ones? Let us pack up and make our way to the king's palace; I'm sure he will make you a lord and me a lady of honour, not to speak of all the fine clothes and presents we shall have.'

"Scrub thought this excellent reasoning, and their packing up began ; but it was soon found that the cottage contained few things fit for carrying to court. Fairfeather could not think of her wooden bowls, spoons, and trenchers being seen there. Scrub considered his lasts and awls better left behind, as without them, he concluded, no one would suspect him of being a cobbler. So putting on their holiday clothes, Fairfeather took her looking-glass and Scrub his drinking horn, which happened to have a very thin rim of silver, and each carrying a golden leaf carefully wrapped up that none might see it till they reached the palace, the pair set out in great expectation.

"How far Scrub and Fairfeather journeyed I cannot say, but when the sun was high and warm at noon, they came into a wood both tired and hungry.

"'If I had known it was so far to court,' said Scrub, ' I would have brought the end of that barley loaf which we left in the cupboard.'

"'Husband,' said Fairfeather, 'you shouldn't have such mean thoughts : how could one eat barley bread on the way to a palace ? Let us rest ourselves under this tree, and look at our golden leaves to see if they are safe.' In looking at the leaves, and talking of their fine prospects, Scrub and Fairfeather did not perceive that a very thin old woman had slipped from behind the tree, with a long staff in her hand and a great wallet by her side.

"'Noble lord and lady,' she said, ' for I know ye are such by your voices, though my eyes are dim and my hearing none of the sharpest, will ye condescend to tell me where I may find some water to mix a bottle of mead which I carry in my wallet, because it is too strong for me ?'

"As the old woman spoke, she pulled out a large wooden bottle such as shepherds used in the ancient times, corked with leaves rolled together, and having a small wooden cup hanging from its handle.

"'Perhaps ye will do me the favour to taste,' she said. ' It is only made of the best honey. I have also cream cheese, and a wheaten loaf here, if such honourable persons as you would eat the like.'

"Scrub and Fairfeather became very condescending after this speech. They were now sure that there must be some appearance of nobility about them ; besides, they were very hungry, and having hastily wrapped up the golden leaves, they assured the old woman they were not at all proud, notwithstanding the lands and castles they had left behind them in the north country, and would willingly help to lighten the wallet. The old woman could scarcely be persuaded to sit down for pure humility, but at length she did, and before the wallet was half empty, Scrub and Fairfeather firmly believed that there must be something remarkably noble-looking about them. This was not entirely owing to her ingenious discourse. The old woman was a wood-witch; her name was Buttertongue; and all her time was spent in making mead, which, being boiled with curious herbs and spells, had the power of making all who drank it fall asleep and dream with their eyes open. She had two dwarfs of sons; one was named Spy, and the other Pounce. Wherever their mother went they were not far behind; and whoever tasted her mead was sure to be robbed by the dwarfs.

"Scrub and Fairfeather sat leaning against the old tree. The cobbler had a lump of cheese in his hand; his wife held fast a hunch of bread. Their eyes and mouths were both open, but they were dreaming of great grandeur at court, when the old woman raised her shrill voice—

"'What ho, my sons! come here and carry home the harvest.'

"No sooner had she spoken, than the two little dwarfs darted out of the neighbouring thicket.

"'Idle boys!' cried the mother, 'what have ye done to-day to help our living?'

"'I have been to the city,' said Spy, 'and could see nothing. These are hard times for us—everybody minds their business so contentedly since that cobbler came; but here is a leathern doublet which his page threw out of the window; it's of no use, but I brought it to let you see I was not idle.' And he tossed down Spare's doublet, with the merry leaves in it, which he had carried like a bundle on his little back.

"To explain how Spy came by it, I must tell you that the forest was not far from the great city where Spare lived in such high esteem. All things had gone well with the cobbler till the king thought that it was quite unbecoming to see such a worthy man without a servant. His majesty, therefore, to let all men understand his royal favour toward Spare, appointed one of his own pages to wait upon him. The name of this youth was Tinseltoes, and, though he was the seventh of the king's pages, nobody in all the court had grander notions. Nothing could please

him that had not gold or silver about it, and his grandmother feared he would hang himself for being appointed page to a cobbler. As for Spare, if anything could have troubled him, this token of his majesty's kindness would have done it.

"The honest man had been so used to serve himself that the page was always in the way, but his merry leaves came to his assistance; and, to the great surprise of his grandmother, Tinseltoes took wonderfully to the new service. Some said it was because Spare gave him nothing to do but play at bowls all day on the palace-green. Yet one thing grieved the heart of Tinseltoes, and that was his master's leathern doublet, but for it he was persuaded people would never remember that Spare had been a cobbler, and the page took a deal of pains to let him see how unfashionable it was at court; but Spare answered Tinseltoes as he had done the king, and at last, finding nothing better would do, the page got up one fine morning earlier than his master, and tossed the leathern doublet out of the back window into a certain lane where Spy found it, and brought it to his mother.

"'That nasty thing!' said the old woman; 'where is the good in it?'

"By this time, Pounce had taken everything of value from Scrub and Fairfeather—the looking-glass, the silver-rimmed horn, the husband's scarlet coat, the wife's gay mantle, and, above all, the golden leaves, which so rejoiced old Buttertongue and her sons, that they threw the leathern doublet over the sleeping cobbler for a jest, and went off to their hut in the heart of the forest.

"The sun was going down when Scrub and Fairfeather awoke from dreaming that they had been made a lord and a lady, and sat clothed in silk and velvet, feasting with the king in his palace-hall. It was a great disappointment to find their golden leaves and all their best things gone. Scrub tore his hair, and vowed to take the old woman's life, while Fairfeather lamented sore; but Scrub, feeling cold for want of his coat, put on the leathern doublet without asking or caring whence it came.

"Scarcely was it buttoned on when a change came over him; he addressed such merry discourse to Fairfeather, that, instead of lamentations, she made the wood ring with laughter. Both busied themselves in getting up a hut of boughs, in which Scrub kindled a fire with a flint and steel, which, together with his pipe, he had brought unknown to Fairfeather, who had told him the like was never heard of at court. Then they found a pheasant's nest at the root of an old oak, made a meal of roasted eggs, and went to sleep on a heap of long green grass which they had gathered, with nightingales singing all night long in the old trees about them. So it happened that Scrub and Fairfeather stayed day after day in the forest, making their hut larger and more comfortable against the winter, living on wild birds' eggs and berries, and never thinking of their lost golden leaves, or their journey to court.

"In the meantime Spare had got up and missed his doublet. Tinseltoes, of course, said he knew nothing about it. The whole palace was searched, and every servant questioned, till all the court wondered why such a fuss was made about an old leathern doublet. That very day things came back to their old fashion. Quarrels began among the lords, and jealousies among the ladies. The king said his subjects did not pay him half enough taxes, the queen wanted more jewels, the servants took to their old bickerings and got up some new ones. Spare found himself getting wonderfully dull, and very much out of place: nobles began to ask what business a cobbler had at the king's table, and his majesty ordered the palace chronicles to be searched for a precedent. The cobbler was too wise to tell all he had lost with that doublet, but being by this time somewhat familiar with court customs, he proclaimed a reward of fifty gold pieces to any who would bring him news concerning it.

"Scarcely was this made known in the city, when the gates and outer courts of the palace were filled by men, women, and children, some bringing leathern doublets of every cut and colour; some with tales of what they had heard and seen in their walks about the neighbourhood; and so much news concerning all sorts of great people came out of these stories, that lords and ladies ran to the king with complaints of Spare as a speaker of slander; and his majesty, being now satisfied that there was no example in all the palace records of such a retainer, issued a decree banishing the cobbler for ever from court, and confiscating all his goods in favour of Tinseltoes.

"That royal edict was scarcely published before the page was in full possession of his rich chamber, his costly garments, and all the presents the courtiers had given him; while Spare, having no longer the fifty pieces of gold to give, was glad to make his escape out of the back window, for fear of the nobles, who vowed to be revenged on him, and the crowd, who were prepared to stone him for cheating them about his doublet.

"The window from which Spare let himself down with a strong rope, was that from which Tinseltoes had tossed the doublet, and as the cobbler came down late in the twilight, a poor woodman, with a heavy load of fagots, stopped and stared at him in great astonishment.

"'What's the matter, friend?' said Spare. 'Did you never see a man coming down from a back window before?"

"'Why,' said the woodman, 'the last morning I passed here a leathern doublet came out of that very window, and I'll be bound you are the owner of it.'

"'That I am, friend," said the cobbler. 'Can you tell me which way that doublet went?"

"'As I walked on,' said the woodman, 'a dwarf, called Spy, bundled it up and ran off to his mother in the forest.'

"'Honest friend,' said Spare, taking off the last of his fine clothes (a grass-green mantle edged with gold), 'I'll give you this if you will follow the dwarf, and bring me back my doublet.'

"'It would not be good to carry fagots in,' said the woodman. 'But if you want back your doublet, the road to the forest lies at the end of this lane,' and he trudged away.

"Determined to find his doublet, and sure that neither crowd nor courtiers could catch him in the forest, Spare went on his way, and was soon among the tall trees; but neither hut nor dwarf could he see. Moreover, the night came on; the wood was dark and tangled, but here and there the moon shone through its alleys, the great owls flitted about, and the nightingales sang. So he went on, hoping to find some place of shelter. At last the red light of a fire, gleaming through a thicket, led him to the door of a low hut. It stood half open, as if there was nothing to fear, and within he saw his brother Scrub snoring loudly on a bed of grass, at the foot of which lay his own leathern doublet; while Fairfeather, in a kirtle made of plaited rushes, sat roasting pheasants' eggs by the fire.

"'Good evening, mistress,' said Spare, stepping in.

"The blaze shone on him, but so changed was her brother-in-law with his court life, that Fairfeather did not know him, and she answered far more courteously than was her wont.

"'Good evening, master. Whence come ye so late? but speak low, for my good man has sorely tired himself cleaving wood, and is taking a sleep, as you see, before supper.'

"'A good rest to him,' said Spare, perceiving he was not known. "I come from the court for a day's hunting, and have lost my way in the forest.'

THE CHRISTMAS CUCKOO.

"'Sit down and have a share of our supper,' said Fairfeather, 'I will put some more eggs in the ashes; and tell me the news of court—I used to think of it long ago when I was young and foolish.'

"'Did you never go there?' said the cobbler. 'So fair a dame as you would make the ladies marvel.'

"'You are pleased to flatter,' said Fairfeather; 'but my husband has a brother there, and we left our moorland village to try our fortune also. An old woman enticed us with fair words and strong drink at the entrance of this forest, where we fell asleep and dreamt of great things; but when we woke, everything had been robbed from us—my looking-glass, my scarlet cloak, my husband's Sunday coat; and, in place of all, the robbers left him that old leathern doublet, which he has worn ever since, and never was so merry in all his life, though we live in this poor hut.'

"'It is a shabby doublet, that,' said Spare, taking up the garment. and seeing that it was his own, for the merry leaves were still sewed in its lining. 'It would be good for hunting in, however—your husband would be glad to part with it, I dare say, in exchange for this handsome cloak;' and he pulled off the green mantle and buttoned on the doublet, much to Fairfeather's delight, who ran and shook Scrub, crying—

"'Husband! husband! rise and see what a good bargain I have made.'

"Scrub gave one closing snore, and muttered something about the root being hard; but he rubbed his eyes, gazed up at his brother, and said—

"'Spare, is that really you? How did you like the court, and have you made your fortune?'

"'That I have, brother,' said Spare, 'in getting back my own good leathern doublet. Come, let us eat eggs, and rest ourselves here this night. In the morning we will return to our own old hut, at the end of the moorland village where the Christmas Cuckoo will come and bring us leaves.'

"Scrub and Fairfeather agreed. So in the morning they all returned, and found the old hut little the worse for wear and weather. The neighbours came about them to ask the news of court, and see if they had made their fortune. Everybody was astonished to find the three poorer than ever, but somehow they liked to go back to the hut. Spare brought out the lasts and awls he had hidden in a corner; Scrub and he began their old trade, and the whole north country found out that there never were such cobblers.

"They mended the shoes of lords and ladies as well as the common people; everybody was satisfied. Their custom increased from day to day, and all that were disappointed, discontented, or unlucky, came to the hut as in old times, before Spare went to court.

"The rich brought them presents, the poor did them service. The hut itself changed, no one knew how. Flowering honeysuckle grew over its roof; red and white roses grew thick about its door. Moreover, the Christmas Cuckoo always came on the first of April, bringing three leaves of the merry tree—for Scrub and Fairfeather would have no more golden ones. So it was with them when I last heard the news of the north country."

The Lords of the White and Grey Castles.

"ONCE upon a time there lived two noble lords in the east country. Their lands lay between a broad river and an old oak forest, whose size was so great that no man knew it. In the midst of his land each lord had a stately castle; one was built of the white freestone, the other of the grey granite. So the one was called Lord of the White Castle, and the other Lord of the Grey.

"There were no lords like them in all the east country for nobleness and bounty. Their tenants lived in peace and plenty; all strangers were hospitably entertained at their castles; and every autumn they sent men with axes into the forest to hew down the great trees, and chop them up into firewood for the poor. Neither hedge nor ditch divided their lands, but these lords never disputed. They had been friends from their youth. Their ladies had died long ago, but the Lord of the Grey Castle had a little son, and the Lord of the White a little daughter; and when they feasted in each other's halls it was their custom to say, 'When our children grow up they will marry,

Don't tell
Anybody.

and have our castles and our lands, and keep our friendship in memory.'

"So the lords and their little children, and tenants, lived happily till one Michaelmas night, as they were all feasting in the hall of the White Castle, there came a traveller to the gate, who was welcomed and feasted as usual. He had seen many strange sights and countries, and, like most people, he liked to tell his travels. The lords were delighted with his tales, as they sat round the fire drinking wine after supper, and at length the Lord of the White Castle, who was very curious, said—

"'Good stranger, what was the greatest wonder you ever saw in all your travels?'

"'The most wonderful sight that ever I saw,' replied the traveller, 'was at the end of yonder forest, where in an ancient wooden house there sits an old woman weaving her own hair into grey cloth on an old crazy loom. When she wants more yarn she cuts off her own grey hair, and it grows so quickly that though I saw it cut in the morning, it was out of the door before noon. She told me it was her purpose to sell the cloth, but none of all who came that way had yet bought any, she asked so great a price; and, only the way is so long and dangerous through that wide forest full of boars and wolves, some rich lord like you might buy it for a mantle.'

"All who heard this story were astonished; but when the traveller had gone on his way the Lord of the White Castle could neither eat nor sleep for wishing to see the old woman that wove her own hair. At length he made up his mind to explore the forest in search of her ancient house, and told the Lord of the Grey Castle his intention. Being a prudent man, this lord replied that traveller's tales were not always to be trusted, and earnestly advised him against undertaking such a long and dangerous journey, for few that went far into that forest ever returned. However, when the curious lord would go in spite of all, he vowed to bear him company for friendship's sake, and they agreed to set out privately, lest the other lords of the land might laugh at them. The Lord of the White Castle had a steward who had served him many years, and his name was Reckoning Robin. To him he said—

"'I am going on a long journey with my friend. Be careful of my goods, deal justly with my tenants, and above all things be kind to my little daughter Loveleaves till my return;' and the steward answered—

"'Be sure, my lord, I will.'

"The Lord of the Grey Castle also had a steward who had served him many years, and his name was Wary Will. To him he said—

"'I am going on a journey with my friend. Be careful of my

goods, deal justly with my tenants, and above all things be kind to my little son Woodwender till my return;' and his steward answered him—

"'Be sure, my lord, I will.'

"So these lords kissed their children while they slept, and set out each with his staff and mantle before sunrise through the old oak forest. The children missed their fathers, the tenants missed their lords. None but the stewards could tell what had become of them; but seven months wore away, and they did not come back. The lords had thought their stewards faithful, because they served so well under their eyes; but instead of that, both were proud and crafty, and thinking that some evil had happened to their masters, they set themselves to be lords in their room.

"Reckoning Robin had a son called Hardhold, and Wary Will, a daughter called Drypennny. There was not a sulkier girl or boy in the country, but their fathers resolved to make a young lord and lady of them; so they took the silk clothes which Woodwender and Love-leaves used to wear, to dress them, clothing the lords' children in frieze and canvas. Their garden flowers and ivory toys were given to Hard-hold and Drypenny; and at last the stewards' children sat at the chief tables, and slept in the best chambers, while Woodwender and Love-leaves were sent to herd the swine and sleep on straw in the granary.

"The poor children had no one to take their part. Every morning at sunrise they were sent out—each with a barley loaf and a bottle of sour milk, which was to serve them for breakfast, dinner, and supper—to watch a great herd of swine on a wide unfenced pasture hard by the forest. The grass was scanty, and the swine were continually straying into the wood in search of acorns; the children knew that if they were lost the wicked stewards would punish them, and between gathering and keeping their herds in order, they were readier to sleep on the granary straw at night than ever they had been within their own silken curtains. Still Woodwender and Loveleaves helped and comforted each other, saying their fathers would

come back, or God would send them some friends: so, in spite of swine-herding and hard living, they looked blithe and handsome as ever; while Hardhold and Drypenny grew crosser and uglier every day, notwithstanding their fine clothes and the best of all things.

"The crafty stewards did not like this. They thought their children ought to look genteel, and Woodwender and Loveleaves like young swineherds; so they sent them to a wilder pasture, still nearer the forest, and gave them two great black hogs, more unruly than all the rest, to keep. One of these hogs belonged to Hardhold, and the other to Drypenny. Every evening when they came home the steward's children used to come down and feed them, and it was their delight to reckon up what price they would bring when properly fattened.

"One sultry day, about midsummer, Woodwender and Loveleaves sat down in the shadow of a mossy rock: the swine grazed about them more quietly than usual, and they plaited rushes and talked to each other, till, as the sun was sloping down the sky, Woodwender saw that the two great hogs were missing. Thinking they must have gone to the forest, the poor children ran to search for them. They heard the thrush singing and the wood-doves calling; they saw the squirrels leaping from bough to bough, and the great deer bounding by; but though they searched for hours, no trace of the favourite hogs could be seen. Loveleaves and Woodwender durst not go home without them. Deeper and deeper they ran into the forest, searching and calling, but all in vain; and when the woods began to darken with the fall of evening, the children feared they had lost their way.

"It was known that they never feared the forest, nor all the boars and wolves that were in it; but being weary, they wished for some place of shelter, and took a green path through the trees, thinking it might lead to the dwelling of some hermit or forester. A fairer way Woodwender and Loveleaves had never walked. The grass was soft and mossy, a hedge of wild roses and honeysuckle grew on either side, and the red light of sunset streamed through the tall trees above. On they went, and it led them straight to a great open dell, covered with the loveliest flowers, bordered with banks of wild strawberries, and all overshadowed by one enormous oak, whose like had never been seen in grove or forest. Its branches were as large as full-grown trees. Its trunk was wider than a country church, and its height like that of a castle. There were mossy seats at its great root, and when the tired

children had gathered as many strawberries as they cared for, they sat down on one, hard by a small spring that bubbled up as clear as crystal. The huge oak was covered with thick ivy, in which thousands of birds had their nests. Woodwender and Loveleaves watched them flying home from all parts of the forest, and at last they saw a lady coming by the same path which led them to the dell. She wore a gown of russet colour; her yellow hair was braided and bound with a crimson fillet. In her right hand she carried a holly branch; but the most remarkable part of her attire was a pair of long sleeves, as green as the very grass.

" 'Who are you?' she said, 'that sit so late beside my well?' and the children told her their story, how they had first lost the hogs, then their way, and were afraid to go home to the wicked stewards.

" 'Well,' said the lady, 'ye are the fairest swineherds that ever came this way. Choose whether ye will go home and keep hogs for Hard-hold and Drypenny, or live in the free forest with me.'

" 'We will stay with you,' said the children, 'for we like not keeping swine. Besides, our fathers went through this forest, and we may meet them some day coming home.'

" While they spoke, the lady slipped her holly branch through the ivy, as if it had been a key—presently a door opened in the oak, and there was a fair house. The windows were of rock crystal, but they could not be seen from without. The walls and floor were covered with thick green moss, as soft as velvet. There were low seats and a round table, vessels of carved wood, a hearth inlaid with curious stones, an oven, and a store chamber for provisions against the winter. When they stepped in, the lady said—

" 'A hundred years have I lived here, and my name is Lady Greensleeves. No friend or servant have I had except my dwarf Corner, who comes to me at the end of harvest with his handmill, his pannier, and his axe: with these he grinds the nuts, and gathers the berries, and cleaves the firewood, and blithely we live all the winter. But Corner loves the frost and fears the sun, and when the topmost boughs begin to bud, he returns to his country far in the north, so I am lonely in the summer time.'

" By this discourse the children saw how welcome they were. Lady Greensleeves gave them deer's milk and cakes of nut-flour, and soft green moss to sleep on; and they forgot all their troubles, the wicked stewards, and the straying swine. Early in the morning a troop of does came to be milked, fairies brought flowers, and birds brought berries, to show Lady Greensleeves what had bloomed and ripened. She taught the children to make cheese of the does' milk, and wine of the wood-berries. She showed them the stores of honey which wild bees had made, and left in hollow trees, the rarest plants of the forest, and the herbs that made all its creatures tame.

"All that summer Woodwender and Loveleaves lived with her in the great oak-tree, free from toil and care; and the children would have been happy, but they could hear no tidings of their fathers. At last the leaves began to fade, and the flowers to fall; Lady Greensleeves said that Corner was coming; and one moonlight night she heaped sticks on the fire, and set her door open, when Woodwender and Loveleaves were going to sleep, saying she expected some old friends to tell her the news of the forest.

"Loveleaves was not quite so curious as her father, the Lord of the White Castle: but she kept awake to see what would happen, and terribly frightened the little girl was when in walked a great brown bear.

"'Good evening, lady,' said the bear.

"'Good evening, bear,' said Lady Greensleeves. 'What is the news in your neighbourhood?'

"'Not much,' said the bear; 'only the fawns are growing very cunning—one can't catch above three in a day.'

"'That's bad news,' said Lady Greensleeves; and immediately in walked a great wild cat.

"'Good evening, lady,' said the cat.

"'Good evening, cat,' said Lady Greensleeves. 'What is the news in your neighbourhood?'

"'Not much,' said the cat; 'only the birds are growing very plentiful—it is not worth one's while to catch them.'

"'That's good news,' said Lady Greensleeves; and in flew a great black raven.

"'Good evening, lady,' said the raven.

"'Good evening, raven,' said Lady Greensleeves. 'What is the news in your neighbourhood?'

"'Not much,' said the raven; 'only in a hundred years or so we shall be very genteel and private—the trees will be so thick.'

"'How is that?' said Lady Green-sleeves.

"'Oh!' said the raven, 'have you not heard how the king of the forest fairies laid a spell on two noble lords, who were travelling through his dominions to see the old woman that weaves her own hair? They had thinned his oaks every year, cutting firewood for the poor: so the king met them in the likeness of a hunter, and asked them to drink out of his oaken goblet, because the day was warm ; and when the two lords drank, they forgot their lands and their tenants, their castles and their children, and minded nothing in all this world but the planting of acorns, which they do day and night, by the power of the spell, in the heart of the forest, and will never cease till some one makes them pause in their work before the sun sets, and then the spell will be broken.'

" 'Ah !' said Lady Greensleeves, 'he is a great prince, that king of the forest fairies; and there is worse work in the world than planting acorns.'

" Soon after, the bear, the cat, and the raven, bade Lady Greensleeves good night. She closed the door, put out the light, and went to sleep on the soft moss as usual.

" In the morning Loveleaves told Woodwender what she had heard, and they went to Lady Greensleeves where she milked the does, and said—

" 'We heard what the raven told last night, and we know the two lords are our fathers : tell us how the spell may be broken !'

" ' I fear the king of the forest fairies,' said Lady Greensleeves, 'because I live here alone, and have no friend but my dwarf Corner ; but I will tell you what you may do. At the end of the path which leads from this dell turn your faces to the north, and you will find a narrow way sprinkled over with black feathers—keep that path, no matter how it winds, and it will lead you straight to the ravens' neighbourhood, where you will find your fathers planting acorns under the forest trees. Watch till the sun is near setting, and tell them the most wonderful things you know to make them forget their work ; but be sure to tell nothing but truth, and drink nothing but running water, or you will fall into the power of the fairy king.'

" The children thanked her for this good council. She packed up cakes and cheese for them in a bag of woven grass, and they soon found the narrow way sprinkled over with black feathers. It was very long, and wound through the thick trees in so many circles that the children were often weary, and sat down to rest. When the night came, they found a mossy hollow in the trunk of an old tree, where they laid themselves down, and slept all the summer night—for Woodwender and Loveleaves never feared the forest. So they went, eating their cakes and cheese when they were hungry, drinking from the running stream, and sleeping in the hollow trees, till on the evening of the seventh day they came into the ravens' neighbourhood. The tall trees were laden with nests and black with ravens. There was nothing to be heard but continual cawing ; and in a great opening where the oaks grew thinnest, the children saw their own fathers busy planting acorns. Each lord had on the velvet mantle in which he left his castle, but it was worn to rags

with rough work in the forest. Their hair and beards had grown long; their hands were soiled with earth; each had an old wooden spade, and on all sides lay heaps of acorns. The children called them by their names, and ran to kiss them, each saying—'Dear father, come back to your castle and your people!' but the lords replied—

"'We know of no castles and no people. There is nothing in all this world but oak-trees and acorns.'

"Woodwender and Loveleaves told them of all their former state in vain—nothing would make them pause for a minute: so the poor children first sat down and cried, and then slept on the cold grass, for the sun set, and the lords worked on. When they awoke it was broad day; Woodwender cheered up his sister, saying—'We are hungry, and there are still two cakes in the bag, let us share one of them—who knows but something may happen?'

"So they divided the cake, and ran to the lords, saying—'Dear fathers, eat with us:' but the lords said—

"There is no use for meat or drink. Let us plant our acorns.'

"Loveleaves and Woodwender sat down, and ate that cake in great sorrow. When they had finished, both went to a stream hard by, and began to drink the clear water with a large acorn shell; and as they drank there came through the oaks a gay young hunter, his mantle was green as the grass: about his neck there hung a crystal bugle, and in his hand he carried a huge oaken goblet, carved with flowers and leaves, and rimmed with crystal. Up to the brim it was filled with milk, on which the rich cream floated; and as the hunter came near, he said—'Fair children, leave that muddy water, and come and drink with me;' but Woodwender and Loveleaves answered—

"'Thanks, good hunter; but we have promised to drink nothing but running water.' Still the hunter came nearer with his goblet, saying—

"'The water is foul: it may do for swineherds and woodcutters, but not for such fair children as you. Tell me, are you not the children of mighty kings? Were you not reared in palaces?' But the boy and girl answered him—

"'No: we were reared in castles, and are the children of yonder lords; tell us how the spell that is upon them may be broken!' and immediately the hunter turned from them with an angry look, poured out the milk upon the ground and went away with his empty goblet.

"Loveleaves and Woodwender were sorry to see the rich cream spilled, but they remembered Lady Greensleeves' warning and seeing they could do no better, each got a withered branch and began to help the lords, scratching up the ground with the sharp end, and planting acorns; but their fathers took no notice of them, nor all that they could say; and when the sun grew warm at noon, they went again to drink at the running stream. Then there came through the oaks another hunter, older than the first, and clothed in yellow: about his neck there hung a silver bugle, and in his hand he carried an oaken goblet, carved with leaves and fruit, rimmed with silver, and filled with mead to the brim. This hunter also asked them to drink, told them the stream was full of frogs, and asked them if they were not a young prince and princess dwelling in the woods for their pleasure? But when Woodwender and Loveleaves answered as before—'We have promised to drink only running water, and are the children of yonder lords: tell us how the spell may be broken!'—he turned from them with an angry look, poured out the mead, and went his way.

"All that afternoon the children worked beside their fathers, planting acorns with the withered branches; but the lords would mind neither them nor their words. And when the evening drew near they were very hungry; so the children divided their last cake, and when no persuasion would make the lords eat with them, they went to the banks of the stream, and began to eat and drink, though their hearts were heavy.

"The sun was getting low, and the ravens were coming home to their nests in the high trees; but one, that seemed old and weary, alighted near them to drink at the stream. As they ate the raven lingered, and picked up the small crumbs that fell.

"'Brother,' said Loveleaves, 'this raven is surely hungry; let us give it a little bit, though it is our last cake.'

"Woodwender agreed, and each gave a bit to the raven; but its great bill finished the morsels in a moment, and hopping nearer, it looked them in the face by turns.

"'The poor raven is still hungry,' said Woodwender, and he gave it another bit. When that was gobbled, it came to Loveleaves, who gave it a bit too, and so on till the raven had eaten the whole of their last cake.

"'Well,' said Woodwender, 'at least, we can have a drink.' But as they stooped to the water, there came through the oaks another hunter, older than the last, and clothed in scarlet: about his neck there hung a golden bugle, and in his hand he carried a huge oaken goblet, carved with ears of corn and clusters of grapes, rimmed with gold, and filled to the brim with wine. He also said—

"'Leave this muddy water, and drink with me. It is full of toads, and not fit for such fair children. Surely ye are from fairyland, and were reared in its queen's palace!' But the children said—

"'We will drink nothing but this water, and yonder lords are our fathers: tell us how the spell may be broken!' And the hunter turned from them with an angry look, poured out the wine on the grass, and went his way. When he was gone, the old raven looked up into their faces, and said—

"'I have eaten your last cake, and I will tell you how the spell may be broken. Yonder is the sun, going down behind yon western trees. Before it sets, go to the lords, and tell them how their stewards used you, and made you herd hogs for Hardhold and Drypenny. When you see them listening, catch up their wooden spades, and keep them if you can till the sun goes down.'

"Woodwender and Loveleaves thanked the raven, and where it flew they never stopped to see, but running to the lords began to tell as they were bidden. At first the lords would not listen, but as the children related how they had been made to sleep on straw, how they had been sent to herd hogs in the wild pasture, and what trouble they had with the unruly swine, the acorn planting grew slower, and at last they dropped their spades.

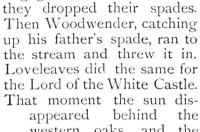

Then Woodwender, catching up his father's spade, ran to the stream and threw it in. Loveleaves did the same for the Lord of the White Castle. That moment the sun disappeared behind the western oaks, and the lords stood up, looking, like men just awoke, on the forest, on the sky, and on their children.

"So this strange story has ended, for Woodwender and Loveleaves went home rejoicing with their fathers. Each lord returned to his castle, and all their tenants made merry. The fine toys and the silk clothes, the flower-gardens and the best chambers, were taken from Hardhold and Drypenny, for the lords' children got them again; and the wicked stewards, with their

cross boy and girl, were sent to herd swine, and live in huts in the wild pasture, which everybody said became them better. The Lord of the White Castle never again wished to see the old woman that wove her own hair, and the Lord of the Grey Castle continued to be his friend. As for Woodwender and Loveleaves, they met with no more misfortunes, but grew up, and were married, and inherited the two castles and the broad lands of their fathers. Nor did they forget the lonely Lady Greensleeves, for it was known in the east country that she and her dwarf Corner always came to feast with them in the Christmas time, and at midsummer they always went to live with her in the great oak in the forest."

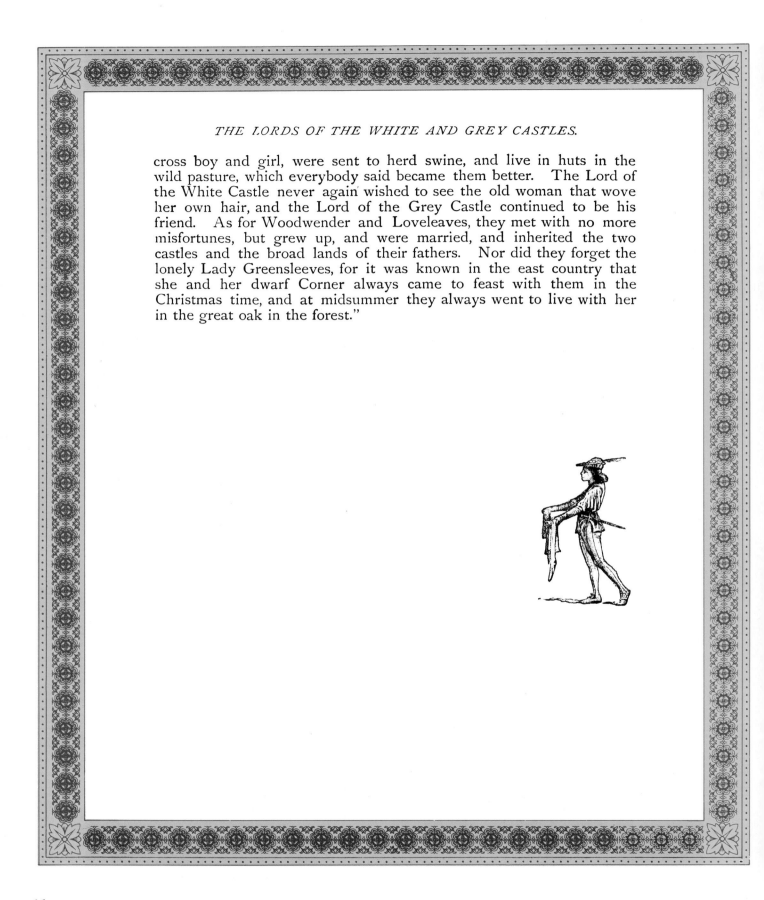

The Greedy Shepherd.

"ONCE upon a time there lived in the south country two
brothers, whose business it was to keep sheep on a great
grassy plain, which was bounded on the one side by a forest,
and on the other by a chain of high hills. No one lived on
that plain but shepherds, who dwelt in low cottages thatched with
heath, and watched their sheep so carefully that no lamb was ever lost,
nor had one of the shepherds ever travelled beyond the foot of the hills
and the skirts of the forest.

"There were none among them more careful than these two
brothers, one of whom was called Clutch, and the other Kind. Though
brethren born, two men of distant countries could not be more unlike
in disposition. Clutch thought of nothing in this world but how to
catch and keep some profit for himself, while Kind would have shared
his last morsel with a hungry dog. This covetous mind made Clutch
keep all his father's sheep when the old man was dead and gone,
because he was the eldest brother, allowing Kind nothing but the place
of a servant to help him in looking after them. Kind wouldn't quarrel
with his brother for the sake of the sheep, so he helped him to keep
them, and Clutch had all his own way. This made him agreeable.
For some time the brothers lived peaceably in their father's cottage,
which stood low and lonely under the shadow of a great sycamore-tree,
and kept their flock with pipe and crook on the grassy plain, till new
troubles arose through Clutch's covetousness.

"On that plain there was neither town, nor city, nor market-place,
where people might sell or buy, but the shepherds cared little for trade.
The wool of their flocks made them clothes; their milk gave them
butter and cheese. At feast times every family killed a lamb or so;
their fields yielded them wheat for bread. The forest supplied them
with firewood for winter; and every midsummer, which is the sheep-
shearing time, traders from a certain far-off city came through it by an
ancient way to purchase all the wool the shepherds could spare, and
give them in exchange either goods or money.

"One midsummer it so happened that these traders praised the
wool of Clutch's flock above all they found on the plain, and gave him

the highest price for it.   That was an unlucky happening for the sheep : from thenceforth Clutch thought he could never get enough wool off them.   At the shearing time nobody clipped so close, and, in spite of all Kind could do or say, he left the poor sheep as bare as if they had been shaven ; and as soon as the wool grew long enough to keep them warm, he was ready with the shears again—no matter how chilly might be the days, or how near the winter.   Kind didn't like these doings, and many a debate they caused between him and his brother.   Clutch always tried to persuade him that close clipping was good for the sheep, and Kind always strove to make him think he had got all the wool— so they were never done with disputes. Still Clutch sold the wool, and stored up his profits, and one midsummer after another passed.   The shepherds began to think him a rich man, and close clipping might have become the fashion, but for a strange thing which happened to his flock.

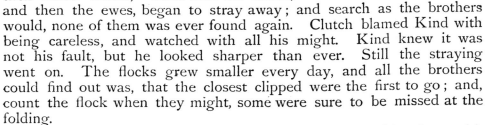

" The wool had grown well that summer. He had taken two crops off them, and was thinking of a third,—though the misty mornings of autumn were come, and the cold evenings made the shepherds put on their winter cloaks,—when first the lambs, and then the ewes, began to stray away ; and search as the brothers would, none of them was ever found again.   Clutch blamed Kind with being careless, and watched with all his might.   Kind knew it was not his fault, but he looked sharper than ever.   Still the straying went on.   The flocks grew smaller every day, and all the brothers could find out was, that the closest clipped were the first to go ; and, count the flock when they might, some were sure to be missed at the folding.

" Kind grew tired of watching, and Clutch lost his sleep with vexation.   The other shepherds, over whom he had boasted of his wool and his profits, were not sorry to see pride having a fall.   Most of them pitied Kind, but all of them agreed that they had marvellous ill luck, and kept as far from them as they could for fear of sharing it. Still the flock melted away as the months wore on.   Storms and cold weather never stopped them from straying, and when the spring came back nothing remained with Clutch and Kind but three old ewes, the

quietest and lamest of their whole flock. They were watching these ewes one evening, in the primrose time, when Clutch, who had never kept his eyes off them that day, said—

"'Brother, there is wool to be had on their backs.'

"'It is too little to keep them warm,' said Kind. 'The east wind still blows sometimes—' but Clutch was off to the cottage for the bag and shears.

"Kind was grieved to see his brother so covetous, and to divert his mind he looked up at the great hills : it was a sort of comfort to him, ever since their losses began, to look at them evening and morning. Now their far-off heights were growing crimson with the setting sun, but as he looked, three creatures like sheep scoured up a cleft in one of them as fleet as any deer : and when Kind turned, he saw his brother coming with the bag and shears, but not a single ewe was to be seen. Clutch's first question was, what had become of them ; and when Kind told him what he saw, the eldest brother scolded him with might and main for ever lifting his eyes off them—

"'Much good the hills and the sunset will do us,' said he, 'now that we have not a single sheep. The other shepherds will hardly give us room among them at shearing time or harvest; but for my part, I'll not stay on this plain to be despised for poverty. If you like to come with me, and be guided by my advice, we shall get service somewhere. I have heard my father say that there were great shepherds living in old times beyond the hills; let us go and see if they will take us for sheep-boys.'

"Kind would rather have stayed and tilled his father's wheat-field, hard by the cottage ; but since his eldest brother would go, he resolved to bear him company. Accordingly, next morning Clutch took his bag and shears, Kind took his crook and pipe, and away they went over the plain and up the hills. All who saw them thought that they had lost their senses, for no shepherd had gone there for a hundred years, and nothing was to be seen but wide moorlands, full of rugged rocks, and sloping up, it seemed, to the very sky. Kind persuaded his brother to take the direction the sheep had taken, but the ground was so rough and steep that after two hours' climbing they would gladly have turned back, if it had not been that their sheep were gone, and the shepherds would laugh at them.

THE GREEDY SHEPHERD.

"By noon they came to the stony cleft, up which the three old ewes had scoured like deer; but both were tired, and sat down to rest. Their feet were sore, and their hearts were heavy; but as they sat there, there came a sound of music down the hills, as if a thousand shepherds had been playing on their tops. Clutch and Kind had never heard such music before. As they listened, the soreness passed from their feet, and the heaviness from their hearts; and getting up, they followed the sound up the cleft, and over a wide heath, covered with purple bloom; till, at sunset, they came to the hill-top, and saw a broad pasture, where violets grew thick among the grass, and thousands of snow-white sheep were feeding, while an old man sat in the midst of them, playing on his pipe. He wore a long coat, the colour of the holly leaves; his hair hung to his waist, and his beard to his knees; but both were as white as snow, and he had the countenance of one who had led a quiet life, and known no cares nor losses.

"'Good father,' said Kind, for his eldest brother hung back and was afraid, 'tell us what land is this, and where can we find service; for my brother and I are shepherds, and can well keep flocks from straying, though we have lost our own.'

"'These are the hill pastures,' said the old man, 'and I am the ancient shepherd. My flocks never stray, but I have employment for you. Which of you can shear best?'

"'Good father,' said Clutch, taking courage, 'I am the closest shearer in all the plain country: you would not find as much wool as would make a thread on a sheep when I have done with it.'

"'You are the man for my business,' replied the old shepherd. 'When the moon rises, I will call the flock you have to shear. Till then sit down and rest, and take your supper out of my wallet.'

"Clutch and Kind gladly sat down by him among the violets, and, opening a leathern bag which hung by his side, the old man gave them cakes and cheese, and a horn cup to drink from at a stream hard by. The brothers felt fit for any work after that meal; and Clutch rejoiced in his own mind at the chance he had got for showing his skill with the shears. 'Kind will see how useful it is to cut close,' he thought to himself: but they sat with the old man, telling him the news of the plain, till the sun went down and the moon rose, and all the snow-white sheep gathered and laid themselves down behind him. Then he took his pipe and played a merry tune, when immediately there was heard a great howling, and up the hills came a troop of shaggy wolves, with hair so long that their eyes could scarcely be seen. Clutch would have fled for fear, but the wolves stopped, and the old man said to him—

" ' Rise, and shear—this flock of mine have too much wool on them.'

" Clutch had never shorn wolves before, yet he couldn't think of losing the good service, and went forward with a stout heart; but the first of the wolves showed its teeth, and all the rest raised such a howl the moment he came near them, that Clutch was glad to throw down his shears, and run behind the old man for safety—

" ' Good father,' cried he, ' I will shear sheep, but not wolves.'

" ' They must be shorn,' said the old man, ' or you go back to the plains, and them after you; but whichever of you can shear them will get the whole flock.'

" On hearing this, Clutch began to exclaim on his hard fortune, and his brother who had brought him there to be hunted and devoured by wolves; but Kind, thinking that things could be no worse, caught up the shears he had thrown away in his fright, and went boldly up to the nearest wolf. To his great surprise, the wild creature seemed to know him, and stood quietly to be shorn, while the rest of the flock gathered round as if waiting their turn. Kind clipped neatly, but not too close, as he had wished his brother to do with the sheep, and heaped up the hair on one side. When he had done with one, another came forward, and Kind went on shearing by the bright moonlight till the whole flock were shorn. Then the old man said—

" ' Ye have done well, take the wool and the flock for your wages, return with them to the plain, and if you please, take this little-worth brother of yours for a boy to keep them.'

" Kind did not much like keeping wolves, but before he could make answer, they had all changed into the very sheep which had strayed away so strangely. All of them had grown fatter and thicker of fleece, and the hair he had cut off lay by his side, a heap of wool so fine and soft that its like had never been seen on the plain.

" Clutch gathered it up in his empty bag, and glad was he to go back to the plain with his brother; for the old man sent them away with their flock, saying no man might see the dawn of day on that pasture but himself, for it was the ground of the fairies. So Clutch and Kind went home with great gladness. All the shepherds came to hear their wonderful story, and ever after liked to keep near them because they had such good luck. They keep the sheep together till this day, but Clutch has grown less greedy, and Kind alone uses the shears."

The Story of Fairyfoot.

"ONCE upon a time there stood far away in the west country a town called Stumpinghame. It contained seven windmills, a royal palace, a market place, and a prison, with every other convenience befitting the capital of a kingdom. A capital city was Stumpinghame, and its inhabitants thought it the only one in the world. It stood in the midst of a great plain, which for three leagues round its walls was covered with corn, flax, and orchards. Beyond that lay a great circle of pasture land, seven leagues in breadth, and it was bounded on all sides by a forest so thick and old that no man in Stumpinghame knew its extent; and the opinion of the learned was, that it reached to the end of the world.

"There were strong reasons for this opinion. First, that forest was known to be inhabited time out of mind by the fairies, and no hunter cared to go beyond its borders—so all the west country believed it to be solidly full of old trees to the heart. Secondly, the people of Stumpinghame were no travellers—man, woman, and child had feet so large and heavy that it was by no means convenient to carry them far. Whether it was the nature of the place or the people, I cannot tell, but great feet had been the fashion there time immemorial, and the higher the family the larger were they. It was, therefore, the aim of everybody above the degree of shepherds, and such-like rustics, to swell out and enlarge their feet by way of gentility; and so successful were they in these undertakings that, on a pinch, respectable people's slippers would have served for panniers.

"Stumpinghame had a king of its own, and his name was Stiffstep; his family was very ancient and large-footed. His subjects called him Lord of the World, and he made a speech to them every year concerning the grandeur of his mighty empire. His

74

queen, Hammerheel, was the greatest beauty in Stumpinghame. Her majesty's shoe was not much less than a fishing-boat; their six children promised to be quite as handsome, and all went well with them till the birth of their seventh son.

" For a long time nobody about the palace could understand what was the matter—the ladies-in-waiting looked so astonished, and the king so vexed; but at last it was whispered through the city that the queen's seventh child had been born with such miserably small feet that they resembled nothing ever seen or heard of in Stumpinghame, except the feet of the fairies.

"The chronicles furnished no example of such an affliction ever before happening in the royal family. The common people thought it portended some great calamity to the city; the learned men began to write books about it; and all the relations of the king and queen assembled at the palace to mourn with them over their singular misfortune. The whole court and most of the citizens helped in this mourning, but when it had lasted seven days they all found out it was of no use. So the relations went to their homes, and the people took to their work. If the learned men's books were written, nobody ever read them; and to cheer up the queen's spirits, the young prince was sent privately out to the pasture lands, to be nursed among the shepherds.

"The chief man there was called Fleecefold, and his wife's name was Rough Ruddy. They lived in a snug cottage with their son Blackthorn, and their daughter Brownberry, and were thought great people, because they kept the king's sheep. Moreover, Fleecefold's family were known to be ancient; and Rough Ruddy boasted that she had the largest feet in all the pastures. The shepherds held them in high respect, and it grew still higher when the news spread that the king's seventh son had been sent to their cottage. People came from all quarters to see the young prince, and great were the lamentations over his misfortune in having such small feet.

"The king and queen had given him fourteen names, beginning with Augustus—such being the fashion in that royal family; but the honest country people could not remember so many; besides, his feet were the most remarkable thing about the child, so with one accord they called him Fairyfoot. At first it was feared this might be high-treason, but when no notice was taken by the king or his ministers, the shepherds concluded it was no harm, and the boy never had another name throughout the pastures. At court it was not thought polite to speak of him at all. They did not keep his birthday, and he was never sent for at Christmas, because the queen and her ladies could not bear the sight. Once a year the undermost scullion was sent to see how he did, with a bundle of his next brother's cast-off clothes; and, as the king grew old and cross, it was said he had thoughts of disowning him.

"So Fairyfoot grew in Fleecefold's cottage. Perhaps the country air made him fair and rosy—for all agreed that he would have been a handsome boy but for his small feet, with which nevertheless he learned to walk, and in time to run and to jump, thereby amazing everybody, for such doings were not known among the children of Stumpinghame, The news of court, however, travelled to the shepherds, and Fairyfoot was despised among them. The old people thought him unlucky; the children refused to play with him. Fleecefold was ashamed to have him in his cottage, but he durst not disobey the king's orders. Moreover, Blackthorn wore most of the clothes brought by the scullion. At last, Rough Ruddy found out that the sight of such horrid jumping would make her children vulgar; and, as soon as he was old enough, she sent Fairyfoot every day to watch some sickly sheep that grazed on a wild, weedy pasture, hard by the forest.

"Poor Fairyfoot was often lonely and sorrowful; many a time he wished his feet would grow larger, or that people wouldn't notice them so much; and all the comfort he had was running and jumping by himself in the wild pasture, and thinking that none of the shepherds' children could do the like, for all their pride of their great feet.

"Tired of this sport, he was lying in the shadow of a mossy rock one warm summer's noon, with the sheep feeding around, when a robin, pursued by a great hawk, flew into the old velvet cap which lay on the ground beside him. Fairyfoot covered it up, and the hawk, frightened by his shout, flew away.

"'Now you may go, poor robin!' he said, opening the cap; but instead of the bird, out sprang a little man dressed in russet-brown, and looking as if he were an hundred years old. Fairyfoot could not speak for astonishment, but the little man said—

"'Thank you for your shelter, and be sure I will do as much for you. Call on me if you are ever in trouble, my name is Robin Good-

fellow;' and darting off, he was out of sight in an instant. For days the boy wondered who that little man could be, but he told nobody, for the little man's feet were as small as his own, and it was clear he would be no favourite in Stumpinghame. Fairyfoot kept the story to himself, and at last midsummer came. That evening was a feast among the shepherds. There were bonfires on the hills, and fun in the villages. But Fairyfoot sat alone beside his sheepfold, for the children of his village had refused to let him dance with them about the bonfire, and he had gone there to bewail the size of his feet, which came between him and so many good things. Fairyfoot had never felt so lonely in all his life, and remembering the little man, he plucked up spirit, and cried—

"'Ho! Robin Goodfellow!'

"'Here I am,' said a shrill voice at his elbow; and there stood the little man himself.

"'I am very lonely, and no one will play with me, because my feet are not large enough,' said Fairyfoot.

"'Come then and play with us,' said the little man. 'We lead the merriest lives in the world, and care for nobody's feet; but all companies have their own manners, and there are two things you must mind among us: first, do as you see the rest doing; and secondly, never speak of anything you may hear or see, for we and the people of this country have had no friendship ever since large feet came in fashion.

"'I will do that, and anything more you like,' said Fairyfoot; and the little man taking his hand, led him over the pasture into the forest, and along a mossy path among old trees wreathed with ivy (he never knew how far), till they heard the sound of music, and came upon a meadow where the moon shone as bright as day, and all the flowers of the year—snowdrops, violets, primroses, and cowslips—bloomed together in the thick grass. There were a crowd of little men and women, some clad in russet colour, but far more in green, dancing round a little well as clear as crystal. And under great rose-trees which grew here and there in the meadow, companies were sitting round low tables covered with cups of milk, dishes of honey, and carved wooden flagons filled with clear red wine. The little man led Fairyfoot up to the nearest table, handed him one of the flagons, and said—

"'Drink to the good company!'

"Wine was not very common among the shepherds of Stumpinghame, and the boy had never tasted such drink as that before; for scarcely had it gone down, when he forgot all his troubles—how Blackthorn and Brownberry wore his clothes, how Rough Ruddy sent him to keep the sickly sheep, and the children would not dance with him: in short, he forgot the whole misfortune of his feet, and it seemed to his mind that he was a king's son, and all was well with him. All the little people about the well cried—

"'Welcome! welcome!' and every one said—'Come and dance with me!' So Fairyfoot was as happy as a prince, and drank milk and ate honey till the moon was low in the sky, and then the little man took him by the hand, and never stopped nor stayed till he was at his own bed of straw in the cottage corner.

"Next morning Fairyfoot was not tired for all his dancing. Nobody in the cottage had missed him, and he went out with the sheep as usual; but every night all that summer, when the shepherds were safe in bed, the little man came and took him away to dance in the forest. Now he did not care to play with the shepherds' children, nor grieve that his father and mother had forgotten him, but watched the sheep all day singing to himself or plaiting rushes; and when the sun went down, Fairyfoot's heart rejoiced at the thought of meeting that merry company.

"The wonder was that he was never tired nor sleepy, as people are apt to be who dance all night; but before the summer was ended Fairyfoot found out the reason. One night, when the moon was full, and the last of the ripe corn rustling in the fields, Robin Goodfellow came for him as usual, and away they went to the flowery green. The fun there was high, and Robin was in haste. So he only pointed to the carved cup from which Fairyfoot every night drank the clear red wine.

"'I am not thirsty, and there is no use losing time,' thought the boy to himself, and he joined the dance; but never in all his life did Fairyfoot find such hard work as to keep pace with the company. Their feet seemed to move like lightning; the swallows did not fly so fast or turn so quickly. Fairyfoot did his best, for he never gave in easily, but at length his breath and strength being spent, the boy was glad to steal away, and sit down behind a mossy oak, where his eyes closed for very weariness. When he awoke the dance was nearly over, but two little ladies clad in green talked close beside him.

"'What a beautiful boy!' said one of them. 'He is worthy to be a king's son. Only see what handsome feet he has!'

"'Yes,' said the other, with a laugh that sounded spiteful; 'they are just like the feet Princess Maybloom had before she washed them in the Growing Well. Her father has sent far and wide throughout the whole country searching for a doctor to make them small again, but nothing in this world can do it except the water of the Fair Fountain, and none but I and the nightingales know where it is.'

"'One would not care to let the like be known,' said the first little lady : 'there would come such crowds of these great coarse creatures of mankind, nobody would have peace for leagues round. But you will surely send word to the sweet princess!—she was so kind to our birds and butterflies, and danced so like one of ourselves!'

"'Not I, indeed!' said the spiteful fairy. 'Her old skinflint of a father cut down the cedar which I loved best in the whole forest, and made a chest of it to hold his money in ; besides, I never liked the princess—everybody praised her so. But come, we shall be too late for the last dance.'"

Eat, birdies, dear,
   as fast as you're able,
There's lots of crumbs
   on our breakfast table!

The Story of Fairyfoot—(*continued*).

"WHEN they were gone, Fairyfoot could sleep no more with astonishment. He did not wonder at the fairies admiring his feet, because their own were much the same; but it amazed him that Princess Maybloom's father should be troubled at hers growing large. Moreover, he wished to see that same princess and her country, since there were really other places in the world than Stumpinghame.

"When Robin Goodfellow came to take him home as usual he durst not let him know that he had overheard anything; but never was the boy so unwilling to get up as on that morning, and all day he was so weary that in the afternoon Fairyfoot fell asleep with his head on a clump of rushes. It was seldom that any one thought of looking after him and the sickly sheep; but it so happened that towards evening the old shepherd, Fleecefold, thought he would see how things went on in the pastures. The shepherd had a bad temper and a thick staff, and no sooner did he catch sight of Fairyfoot sleeping, and his flock stray-

ing away, than shouting all the ill names he could remember, in a voice which woke up the boy, he ran after him as fast as his great feet would allow; while Fairyfoot, seeing no other shelter from his fury, fled into the forest, and never stopped nor stayed till he reached the banks of a little stream.

"Thinking it might lead him to the fairies' dancing-ground, he followed that stream for many an hour, but it wound away into the heart of the forest, flowing through dells, falling over mossy rocks, and at last leading Fairyfoot, when he was tired and the night had fallen, to a grove of great rose-trees, with the moon shining on it as bright as day, and thousands of nightingales singing in the branches.

THE STORY OF FAIRYFOOT.

In the midst of that grove was a clear spring, bordered with banks of lilies, and Fairyfoot sat down by it to rest himself and listen. The singing was so sweet he could have listened for ever, but as he sat the nightingales left off their songs, and began to talk together in the silence of the night—

"'What boy is that,' said one on a branch above him, 'who sits so lonely by the Fair Fountain? He cannot have come from Stumping-hame with such small and handsome feet.'

"'No, I'll warrant you,' said another, 'he has come from the west country. How in the world did he find the way?'

"'How simple you are!' said a third nightingale. 'What had he to do but follow the ground-ivy which grows over height and hollow, bank and bush, from the lowest gate of the king's kitchen-garden to the root of this rose-tree? He looks a wise boy, and I hope he will keep the secret, or we shall have all the west country here, dabbling in our fountain, and leaving us no rest to either talk or sing.'

"Fairyfoot sat in great astonishment at this discourse, but by and by, when the talk ceased and the songs began, he thought it might be as well for him to follow the ground-ivy, and see the Princess May-bloom, not to speak of getting rid of Rough Ruddy, the sickly sheep, and the crusty old shepherd. It was a long journey; but he went on, eating wild berries by day, sleeping in the hollows of old trees by night, and never losing sight of the ground-ivy, which led him over height and hollow, bank and bush, out of the forest, and along a noble high road, with fields and villages on every side, to a great city, and a low old-fashioned gate of the king's kitchen-garden, which was thought too mean for the scullions, and had not been opened for seven years.

"There was no use knocking—the gate was overgrown with tall weeds and moss; so, being an active boy, he climbed over, and walked through the garden, till a white fawn came frisking by, and he heard a soft voice saying sorrow-fully—

"'Come back, come back, my fawn! I cannot run and play with you now, my feet have grown so heavy;' and looking round he saw the loveliest young princess in the world, dressed in snow-white, and wearing a wreath of roses on her golden hair; but walking slowly, as the great people did in Stumpinghame, for her feet were as large as the best of them.

"After her came six young ladies, dressed in white and walking slowly, for they could not go before the princess; but Fairyfoot was amazed to see that their feet were as small as his own. At once he guessed that this must be the Princess Maybloom, and made her an humble bow, saying—

"'Royal princess, I have heard of your trouble because your feet have grown large: in my country that's all the fashion. For seven years past I have been wondering what would make mine grow, to no purpose; but I know of a certain fountain that will make yours smaller and finer than ever they were, if the king, your father, gives you leave to come with me, accompanied by two of your maids that are the least given to talking, and the most prudent officer in all his household; for it would grievously offend the fairies and the nightingales to make that fountain known.'

"When the princess heard that, she danced for joy in spite of her large feet, and she and her six maids brought Fairyfoot before the king and queen, where they sat in their palace hall, with all the courtiers paying their morning compliments. The lords were very much astonished to see a ragged, bare-footed boy brought in among them, and the ladies thought Princess Maybloom must have gone mad; but Fairyfoot, making an humble reverence, told his message to the king and queen, and offered to set out with the princess that very day. At first the king would not believe that there could be any use in his offer, because so many great physicians had failed to give any relief. The courtiers laughed Fairyfoot to scorn, the pages wanted to turn him out for an impudent impostor, and the prime-minister said he ought to be put to death for high-treason.

"Fairyfoot wished himself safe in the forest again, or even keeping the sickly sheep; but the queen, being a prudent woman, said—

"'I pray your majesty to notice what fine feet this boy has. There may be some truth in his story. For the sake of our only daughter, I will choose two maids who talk the least of all our train, and my chamberlain, who is the most discreet officer in our household. Let them go with the princess: who knows but our sorrow may be lessened?'

"After some persuasion the king consented, though all his councillors advised the contrary. So the two silent maids, the discreet chamberlain, and her fawn, which would not stay behind, were sent with Princess Maybloom, and they all set out after dinner. Fairyfoot had hard work guiding them along the track of the ground-ivy. The maids and the chamberlain did not like the brambles and rough roots of the forest —they thought it hard to eat berries and sleep in hollow trees; but the

THE STORY OF FAIRYFOOT.

Princess went on with good courage, and at last they reached the grove of rose-trees, and the spring bordered with lilies.

" The chamberlain washed—and though his hair had been grey, and his face wrinkled, the young courtiers envied his beauty for years after. The maids washed—and from that day they were esteemed the fairest in all the palace. Lastly, the princess washed also—it could make her no fairer, but the moment her feet touched the water they grew less, and when she had washed and dried them three times, they were as small and finely-shaped as Fairyfoot's own. There was great joy among them, but the boy said sorrowfully—

" ' Oh ! if there had been a well in the world to make my feet large, my father and mother would not have cast me off, nor sent me to live among the shepherds.'

" ' Cheer up your heart,' said the Princess Maybloom ; ' if you want large feet, there is a well in this forest that will do it. Last summer time, I came with my father and his foresters to see a great cedar cut down, of which he meant to make a money chest. While they were busy with the cedar, I saw a bramble branch covered with berries. Some were ripe and some were green, but it was the longest bramble that ever grew ; for the sake of the berries, I went on and on to its root, which grew hard by a muddy-looking well, with banks of dark green moss, in the deepest part of the forest. The day was warm and dry, and my feet were sore with the rough ground, so I took off my scarlet shoes, and washed my feet in the well ; but as I washed they grew larger every minute, and nothing could ever make them less again. I have seen the bramble this day ; it is not far off, and as you have shown me the Fair Fountain, I will show you the Growing Well.'

" Up rose Fairyfoot and Princess Maybloom, and went together till they found the bramble, and came to where its root grew, hard by the muddy-looking well, with banks of dark green moss in the deepest dell of the forest. Fairyfoot sat down to wash, but at that minute he heard a sound of music, and knew it was the fairies going to their dancing ground.

" ' If my feet grow large,' said the boy to himself, ' how shall I dance with them ? ' So, rising quickly, he took the Princess Maybloom by the hand. The fawn followed them ; the maids and the chamberlain followed it, and all followed the music through the forest. At last they came to the flowery green. Robin Goodfellow welcomed the company for Fairyfoot's sake, and gave every one a drink of the fairies' wine. So they danced there from sunset till the grey morning, and nobody was tired ; but before the lark sang, Robin Goodfellow took them all safe home, as he used to take Fairyfoot.

" There was great joy that day in the palace because Princess May-

bloom's feet were made small again. The king gave Fairyfoot all manner of fine clothes and rich jewels; and when they heard his wonderful story, he and the queen asked him to live with them and be their son. In process of time Fairyfoot and Princess Maybloom were married, and still live happily. When they go to visit at Stumpinghame, they always wash their feet in the Growing Well, lest the royal family might think them a disgrace, but when they come back, they make haste to the Fair Fountain; and the fairies and the nightingales are great friends to them, as well as the maids and the chamberlain, because they have told nobody about it, and there is peace and quiet yet in the grove of rose-trees."

The Story of Childe Charity.

"ONCE upon a time, there lived in the west country a little girl who had neither father nor mother; they both died when she was very young, and left their daughter to the care of her uncle, who was the richest farmer in all that country. He had houses and lands, flocks and herds, many servants to work about his house and fields, a wife who had brought him a great dowry, and two fair daughters. All their neighbours, being poor, looked up to the family—insomuch that they imagined themselves great people. The father and mother were as proud as peacocks; the daughters thought themselves the greatest beauties in the world, and not one of the family would speak civilly to anybody they thought low.

"Now it happened that though she was their near relation, they had this opinion of the orphan girl, partly because she had no fortune, and partly because of her humble, kindly disposition. It was said that the more needy and despised any creature was, the more ready was she to befriend it: on which account the people of the west country called her Childe Charity, and if she had any other name, I never heard it. Childe Charity was thought very mean in that proud house. Her uncle would not own her for his niece; her cousins would not keep her company; and her aunt sent her to work in the dairy, and to sleep in the back garret, where they kept all sorts of lumber and dry herbs for the winter. All the servants learned the same tune, and Childe Charity had more work than rest among them. All the day she scoured pails, scrubbed dishes, and washed crockeryware; but every night she slept in the back garret as sound as a princess could in her palace chamber.

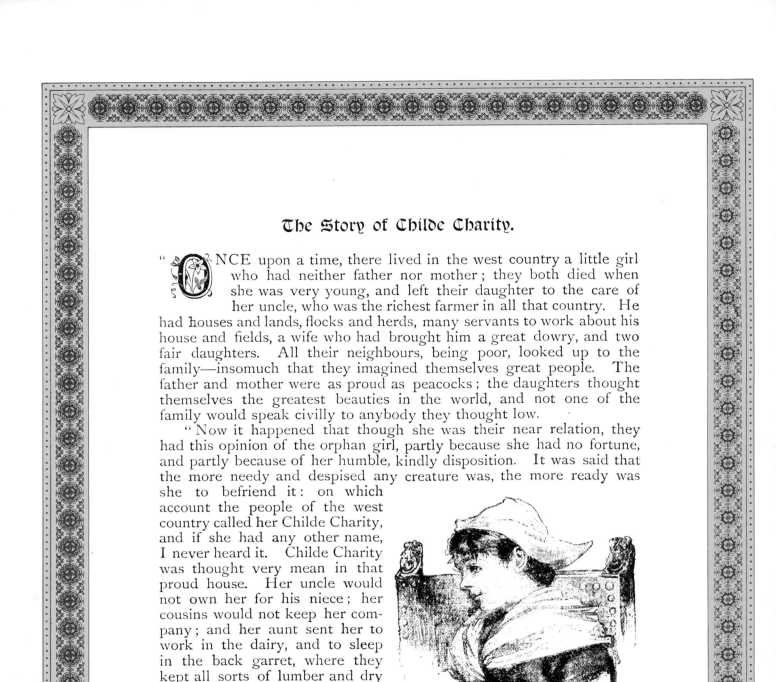

"Her uncle's house was large and white, and stood among green meadows by a river's side. In front it had a porch covered with a vine; behind, it had a farmyard and high granaries. Within, there were two parlours for the rich, and two kitchens for the poor, which the neighbours thought wonderfully grand; and one day in the harvest season, when this rich farmer's corn had been all cut down and housed, he condescended so far as to invite them to a harvest supper. The west country people came in their holiday clothes and best behaviour. Such heaps of cakes and cheese, such baskets of apples and barrels of ale, had never been at feast before; and they were making merry in kitchen and parlour, when a poor old woman came to the backdoor, begging for broken victuals and a night's lodging. Her clothes were coarse and ragged; her hair was scanty and grey; her back was bent; her teeth were gone. She had a squinting eye, a clubbed foot, and crooked fingers. In short, she was the poorest and ugliest old woman that ever came begging. The first who saw her was the kitchen-maid, and she ordered her to be gone for an ugly witch. The next was the herd-boy, and he threw her a bone over his shoulder; but Childe Charity, hearing the noise, came out from her seat at the foot of the lowest table, and asked the old woman to take her share of the supper, and sleep that night in her bed in the back garret. The old woman sat down without a word of thanks. All the company laughed at Childe Charity for giving her bed and her supper to a beggar. Her proud cousins said it was just like her mean spirit, but Childe Charity did not mind them. She scraped the pots for her supper that night, and slept on a sack among the lumber, while the old woman rested in her warm bed; and next morning, before the little girl awoke, she was up and gone, without so much as saying thank you, or good morning.

"That day all the servants were sick after the feast, and mostly cross too—so you may judge how civil they were; when, at supper time, who should come to the backdoor but the old woman, again asking for broken victuals and a night's lodging. No one would listen to her or give her a morsel, till Childe Charity rose from her seat at the foot of the lowest table, and kindly asked her to take her supper, and sleep in her bed in the back garret. Again the old woman sat down without a word. Childe Charity scraped the pots for her supper, and slept on the sack. In the morning the old woman was gone; but for six nights after, as sure as the supper was spread, there was she at the backdoor, and the little girl regularly asked her in.

"Childe Charity's aunt said she would let her get enough of beggars. Her cousins made continual game of what they called her genteel visitor. Sometimes the old woman said, 'Child why don't you make this bed softer? and why are your blankets so thin?' but

90

she never gave her a word of thanks nor a civil good morning. At last, on the ninth night from her first coming, when Childe Charity was getting used to scrape the pots and sleep on the sack, her accustomed knock came to the door, and there she stood with an ugly ashy-coloured dog, so stupid-looking and clumsy that no herd-boy would keep him.

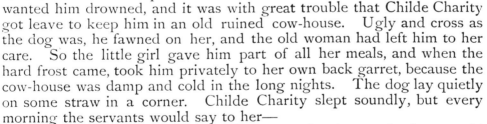

"'Good evening, my little girl,' she said when Childe Charity opened the door, 'I will not have your supper and bed to-night—I am going on a long journey to see a friend ; but here is a dog of mine, whom nobody in all the west country will keep for me. He is a little cross, and not very handsome ; but I leave him to your care till the shortest day in all the year. Then you and I will count for his keeping.'

"When the old woman had said the last word, she set off with such speed that Childe Charity lost sight of her in a minute. The ugly dog began to fawn upon her, but he snarled at everybody else. The servants said he was a disgrace to the house. The proud cousins wanted him drowned, and it was with great trouble that Childe Charity got leave to keep him in an old ruined cow-house. Ugly and cross as the dog was, he fawned on her, and the old woman had left him to her care. So the little girl gave him part of all her meals, and when the hard frost came, took him privately to her own back garret, because the cow-house was damp and cold in the long nights. The dog lay quietly on some straw in a corner. Childe Charity slept soundly, but every morning the servants would say to her—

"'What great light and fine talking was that in your back garret ?'

"'There was no light but the moon shining in through the shutterless window, and no talk that I heard,' said Childe Charity, and she thought they must have been dreaming ; but night after night, when any of them awoke in the dark and silent hour that comes before the morning, they saw a light brighter and clearer than the Christmas fire, and heard voices like those of lords and ladies in the back garret.

"Partly from fear, and partly from laziness, none of the servants would rise to see what might be there ; till at length, when the winter nights were at the longest, the little parlour maid, who did least work and got most favour, because she gathered news for her mistress, crept out of bed when all the rest were sleeping, and set herself to watch at a crevice of the door. She saw the dog lying quietly in the corner, Childe Charity sleeping soundly in her bed, and the moon shining through the shutterless window; but an hour before daybreak there came a glare of lights, and a sound of far-off bugles. The window opened, and in marched a troop of little men clothed in crimson and gold, and bearing every man a torch, till the room looked bright as day. They marched up with great reverence to the dog, where he lay on the straw, and the most richly clothed among them said—

" ' Royal prince, we have prepared the banquet hall. What will your highness please that we do next ? '

" ' Ye have done well,' said the dog. ' Now prepare the feast, and see that all things be in our first fashion : for the princess and I mean to bring a stranger who never feasted in our halls before.'

" ' Your highness's commands shall be obeyed,' said the little man, making another reverence ; and he and his company passed out of the window. By and by there was another glare of lights, and a sound like far-off flutes. The window opened, and there came in a company of little ladies clad in rose-coloured velvet, and carrying each a crystal lamp. They also walked with great reverence up to the dog, and the gayest among them said—

" ' Royal prince, we have prepared the tapestry. What will your highness please that we do next ? '

" ' Ye have done well,' said the dog. ' Now prepare the robes, and let all things be in our first fashion : for the princess and I will bring with us a stranger who never feasted in our halls before.'

" ' Your highness's commands shall be obeyed,' said the little lady, making a low courtesy ; and she and her company passed out through the window, which closed quietly behind them. The dog stretched himself out upon the straw, the little girl turned in her sleep, and the moon shone in on the back garret. The parlour-maid was so much amazed, and so eager to tell this great story to her mistress, that she could not close her eyes that night, and was up before cock-crow ; but when she told it, her mistress called her a silly wench to have such foolish dreams, and scolded her so that the parlour-maid durst not

mention what she had seen to the servants. Nevertheless Childe Charity's aunt thought there might be something in it worth knowing; so next night, when all the house were asleep, she crept out of bed, and set herself to watch at the back garret door. There she saw exactly what the maid told her—the little men with the torches, and the little ladies with the crystal lamps, come in making great reverence to the dog, and the same words pass, only he said to the one, 'Now prepare the presents,' and to the other, 'Prepare the jewels;' and when they were gone the dog stretched himself on the straw, Childe Charity turned in her sleep, and the moon shone in on the back garret.

"The mistress could not close her eyes any more than the maid from eagerness to tell the story. She woke up Childe Charity's rich uncle before cock-crow; but when he heard it, he laughed at her for a foolish woman, and advised her not to repeat the like before the neighbours, lest they should think she had lost her senses. The mistress could say no more, and the day passed; but that night the master thought he would like to see what went on in the back garret: so when all the house were asleep he slipped out of bed, and set himself to watch at the crevice in the door. The same thing happened again that the maid and the mistress saw: the little men in crimson with their torches, and the little ladies in rose-coloured velvet with their lamps, came in at the window, and made an humble reverence to the ugly dog, the one saying, 'Royal prince, we  have prepared the presents,' and the other, 'Royal prince, we have prepared the jewels;' and the dog said to them all, 'Ye have done well. To-morrow come and meet me and the princess with horses and chariots, and let all things be in our first fashion: for we will bring a stranger from this house who has never travelled with us, nor feasted in our halls before.'

"The little men and the little ladies said, 'Your highness's commands shall be obeyed.' When they had gone out through the window, the ugly dog stretched himself out on the straw, Childe Charity turned in her sleep, and the moon shone in on the back garret.

"The master could not close his eyes any more than the maid or the mistress, for thinking of this strange sight. He remembered to have heard his grandfather say, that somewhere near his meadows there lay a path leading to the fairies' country, and the haymakers used to see it shining through the grey summer morning as the fairy bands went home. Nobody had heard or seen the like for many years; but the master concluded that the doings in his back garret must be a fairy business, and the ugly dog a person of great account. His chief wonder was, however, what visitor the fairies intended to take from his house; and after thinking the matter over, he was sure it must be one of his daughters—they were so handsome, and had such fine clothes.

"Accordingly, Childe Charity's rich uncle made it his first business that morning to get ready a breakfast of roast mutton for the ugly dog, and carry it to him in the old cow-house; but not a morsel would the dog taste. On the contrary, he snarled at the master, and would have bitten him if he had not run away with his mutton.

" 'The fairies have strange ways,' said the master to himself; but he called his daughters privately, bidding them dress themselves in their best, for he could not say which of them might be called into great company before nightfall. Childe Charity's proud cousins, hearing this, put on the richest of their silks and laces, and strutted like peacocks from kitchen to parlour all day, waiting for the call their father spoke of, while the little girl scoured and scrubbed in the dairy. They were in very bad humour when night fell, and nobody had come; but just as the family were sitting down to supper the ugly dog began to bark, and the old woman's knock was heard at the backdoor. Childe Charity opened it, and was going to offer her bed and supper as usual, when the old woman said—

" 'This is the shortest day in all the year, and I am going home to hold a feast after my travels. I see you have taken good care of my dog, and now if you will come with me to my house, he and I will do our best to entertain you. Here is our company.'

"As the old woman spoke, there was a sound of far-off flutes and bugles, then a glare of lights; and a great company, clad so grandly that they shone with gold and jewels, came in open chariots, covered with gilding and drawn by snow-white horses. The first and finest of the chariots was empty. The old woman led Childe Charity to it by the hand, and the ugly dog jumped in before her. The proud cousins, in all their finery, had by this time come to the door, but nobody wanted them; and no sooner was the old woman and her dog within the chariot than a marvellous change passed over them, for the ugly old woman turned at once to a beautiful young princess, with long yellow curls and a robe of green and gold, while the ugly dog at her side started up a fair young prince, with nut-brown hair and a robe of purple and silver.

"'We are,' said they, as the chariots drove on, and the little girl sat astonished, 'a prince and princess of Fairyland, and there was a wager between us whether or not there were good people still to be found in these false and greedy times. One said **Yes**, and the other said No; and I have lost,' said the prince, 'and must pay the feast and presents.'

"Childe Charity never heard any more of that story. Some of the farmer's household, who were looking after them through the moonlight night, said the chariots had gone one way across the meadows, some said they had gone another, and till this day they cannot agree upon the direction. But Childe Charity went with that noble company into a country such as she had never seen — for primroses covered all the ground, and the light was always like that of a summer evening. They took her to a royal palace, where there was nothing but feasting and dancing for seven days. She had robes of pale green velvet to wear, and slept in a chamber inlaid with ivory. When the feast was done, the prince and princess gave her such heaps of gold and jewels that she could not carry them, but they gave her a chariot to go home in, drawn by six white horses; and on the seventh night, which happened to be Christmas time, when the farmer's family had settled in their own minds that she would never come back, and were sitting down to supper, they heard the sound of her coachman's bugle, and saw her alight with all the jewels and gold at the very backdoor where she had brought in the ugly old woman. The fairy chariot drove away, and never came back to that farmhouse after. But Childe Charity scrubbed and scoured no more, for she grew a great lady, even in the eyes of her proud cousins."